MENDING IMAGES
with the billionaire

OTHER BOOKS BY LORIN GRACE

Artists & Billionaires 4

MENDING IMAGES
with the billionaire

LORIN GRACE

CURRANT
CREEK PRESS

Cover Design © 2018 LJP Creative
Photos © Deposit Photos, Background photos by Colin Maynard and
Gaby Yu on Unsplash

Formatting by LJP Creative
Edits by Eschler Editing

Published by Currant Creek Press
North Logan, Utah

First edition: October 2018
ISBN: 978-0-9984110-9-5

For Dad
MY FAVORITE PHOTOGRAPHER IN THE WORLD.

ABBIE HASTINGS ADJUSTED ONE OF the filters Mandy had given her until Araceli's eyes danced with joy in the graduation photo on her computer screen. Ever since meeting the women at Friday Night Art Society, Abbie had spent more time on expanding her photography hobby. Learning about lighting and composition as well as a few digital-correction tricks completely changed the world she viewed from behind her camera. Candace and the others in the Art House had always been kind enough to include Abbie in their projects because as Mandy Crawford's principle bodyguard, she usually had to be where Mandy was. But recently, Abbie suspected her inclusion had more to do with friendship than duty. This morning she found herself split between the two options. She should be with Mandy.

Sometime before dawn, her brother Alex had accompanied Mandy and her husband, Daniel, on a nonroutine trip to the maternity ward at the county hospital.

She rechecked her phone. No missed calls. No missed texts.

Her father's warnings had proved correct. She'd become too attached to her client. But who wouldn't fall in love with Mandy?

"Are those Araceli's and Tessa's graduation photos?" Candace pointed over Abbie's shoulder. "They turned out great! I love the one of Araceli and Kyle in front of the bell tower. And, oh, this one of Tessa with Sean—I am so glad he proposed. They make such a good team."

Abbie jumped.

When had Candace come into the room, and how had she missed it? Technically she was off duty, but being distracted wasn't good. She took a deep breath to calm her nerves before answering. "Don't you love this one?" she asked as she enlarged the photo of Araceli hugging her dad.

"I want to frame it and give it to Mr. Williams when we go back for the wedding. Any word on Mandy yet?"

"No, I'm getting worried. I thought someone would text by now. I wish I had stayed at the guard house last night. Then I could have been with them. Mandy's safety is my job."

Candace put her arm around Abbie, the soft pale-pink locks of the wig she'd purchased to celebrate the first Friday Night Art Society baby brushing Abbie's cheek. "I don't think this is something in your job description. You can't round kick the doctor or force the contractions to stop."

"But she is only at thirty-two weeks."

"I know. That's why we prayed together this morning, and I have been texting everyone I can to let them know to pray too. Colin is doing the same. Mandy has many friends, and there is strength in numbers."

Abbie closed her laptop. "I probably should go pack. The little hospital here doesn't have a NICU, so I am sure that whatever happens, Daniel will want to move her back to the Chicago penthouse and her regular OB."

"Only pack what you need. The room is yours as long as you want it. I don't think I could live with another empty room. Have you seen Araceli's? There is carpet in there. I had forgotten what color it was. And with the last of Tessa's stuff gone from the room the two of you've been sharing, the house feels half empty." Candace gave her head a little shake.

"It has felt half empty most of the semester with as much time as Tessa spent in New York."

"Not to complain, but two roommates getting married this summer, both asking me to be their maid of honor is going to keep me busy. I am not sure what Araceli was thinking—only three weeks between graduation and the wedding. Do you know if you're going to Boston yet?"

Mandy wanted to go, but the doctor didn't want her flying. "We looked at the train option. Daniel wants something like the old Pullman cars for Mandy. I think he's leaning toward a luxury bus equipped with a queen bed in it. But—"

Candace finished the thought for Abbie. "It might not happen. Best that Mandy and the baby are safe. The Evans family is arranging to pick up me and Zoe in a private jet. All these billionaires are spoiling me. I'll never be able to go back to real life."

"Are you talking about me again?" Zoe entered from the direction of the library.

"No, I was telling Abbie about our flight." Candace's voice took on a teasing tone as it often did with her younger cousin.

"Oh, so real life means not having expensive travel options?" Zoe crossed to the fridge and pulled out a mineral water.

"Pretty much. Once Araceli and Tessa get married, I'll have four former roommates married to billionaires. Statistically, I bet I have a better chance of being hit by a meteor."

Abbie zipped up her laptop case. "Who is the fourth?"

"My first roommate, Kim, married a chemical genius who invented some formula and bingo! Another rich husband." Candace pulled her phone out and studied the screen before putting it back in her pocket.

Zoe opened her bottle and joined them at the table. "What about you and Colin?"

Candace scowled but was spared answering as the first three cords of Bach's Fugue in B Minor played. Abbie grabbed her phone. "Hello?"

3

"It's Daniel. The good news is they have stopped the contractions. However, even the doctors don't want Mandy at a hospital without a NICU. Our options are to take an ambulance ride to Fort Wayne or hire a private medical transport to Chicago. Mandy's doctor in Chicago wants to keep her on twenty-four-hour monitoring before she sends her home on bed rest."

Abbie didn't need to ask what option Daniel had chosen. "When do you leave for Chicago?"

"Within the hour."

"What do you need me to do?" Abbie started gathering her things.

"You know the two-month paid vacation Mandy promised you after the baby comes in July? Well, your vacation just increased to four starting today. Go have fun and take lots of pictures at Araceli's wedding. Mandy is very firm on the photo part. She is heartbroken about not being able to go."

"So you don't need me?"

"Not as a bodyguard but as Mandy's friend, always. Her mother is flying up from South America, so come and visit as often as you want. The doctor is here. I need to go. I'll have Alex call you, and I know Mandy will soon."

The phone went silent. Abbie relayed the pertinent information to Zoe and Candace. "So is there another spot in Kyle Evans's jet for the wedding? I'm on extended vacation."

The Hastings Security agency was everything Preston T. Harmon expected it to be. The receptionist, middle-aged and professional, was unassuming and most likely armed, well-hidden security cameras monitoring his every move. He suspected that her call to Jethro Hastings to announce his presence was entirely unnecessary. A glint in the receptionist's eye made him think twice about proceeding. Very few people measured a Chicago Harmon and found them lacking, but she did not seem impressed.

He checked his tie before entering the owner's office.

Preston shook the hand of the man behind the desk. Mr. Jethro Hastings could easily win a round of almost anything against half the members of Preston's father's security team. Preston swallowed as he took his seat, knowing he had come to the right place.

"Mr. Harmon—"

"Preston, please. I am always looking for my father, grandfather, or uncle when someone calls me mister."

"I am curious why you are here. Your family has their own private team and a very good one at that."

"Which is part of the problem. I don't know who I can trust. So far our team has come up with very few leads. I have begun to wonder if part of my problem is our men. It's time to go outside our team, and according to Daniel Crawford, you have the best security firm in Chicago."

"You know Mr. Crawford?" Jethro sat back in his chair. Preston guessed the owner to be in his mid-fifties, but other than his short-cropped gray hair and a few wrinkles around the eyes, there was little to pinpoint his age. Mr. Hastings wore a jacket over a tie-less button down, business casual or easier to conceal his shoulder holster, Preston wasn't sure.

Preston hadn't squirmed in his chair this much since he'd sat with Daniel in front of the headmaster at their boarding school when he was seventeen and Daniel thirteen. "We were in school together."

Jethro smiled. "Then we've met before."

"I hoped you wouldn't remember." The tie around his neck tightened. "That was a long time ago."

"So, why are you here? I assume it's for a better reason than talking the younger students into moving the headmaster's 1970 Monte Carlo onto the roof of the gym."

"No, I learned my lesson. I have a problem. My girlfriends and fiancées keep dumping me."

"Have you tried a dating service?"

"No. Finding a date is not my problem. It's the stalker. About three years ago he started terrorizing my girlfriends. Every time I get into a serious relationship, the woman I am dating starts getting threats. They escalate until she dumps me. Last year the stalker scared my fiancée so badly she canceled the wedding and moved to Europe. I am ready to propose to Yvette. I have everything all planned out so we can have a quick wedding. The invitations will be sent out the morning after we announce the proposal, and we will be married a month later. I don't want to give the stalker time to scare her off, too." Preston found he could breathe again.

"Has she received any threats?"

"Just the usual notes and black rose. Our security team intercepted about half of those. All of the roses come from the same florist. A man orders them, and then a courier or Uber driver shows up, pays in cash, and delivers the flowers. The florist has been cooperating with us, but none of the couriers has been able to give us a lead beyond a man orders them by phone. They get the cash from various sources, including an envelope taped to the underside of a table at a McDonald's." He kept his voice even as to not betray his frustration. Order and organization were the hallmarks of his life, a genetic gift from his British mother.

Jethro wrote on a notepad. "Does Yvette know about the threats to your former girlfriends?"

"When things got serious, I told her. She moved into the guesthouse so she could be under our security umbrella."

"So, what do you need?"

"I need a bodyguard no one will recognize and who can blend in. I don't want Yvette to realize she has another one. I don't even want our team to realize Yvette has another guard. Whoever the stalker is, they have gotten onto the property again."

"Again?"

Preston pulled a clear gallon plastic bag out of his pocket. "She found this note on her pillow this morning when she came out of the shower."

"Who's touched it?" Jethro reached for the bag and examined the contents.

"Only Yvette."

"I can't tell you the last time I read a message cut out from magazine letters."

"*Vogue*. At least the V in *violets* is off the index page."

Jethro raised an eyebrow.

Preston shrugged. "Publishing empire. I know my competition's logos."

"Not the best poetry." Jethro read the note. 'Roses are red, violets are blue, only the dead say 'I do.'" He set the note to the side of his desk. "Can you get me Yvette's fingerprints?"

"I'll email them to you. She modeled for us before we started dating, and we took her prints as part of her security check. Yvette is a video blogger who runs a fashion blog and posts all over social media. I think if we get a bodyguard to be a special wedding photographer who follows her every move all month, she will never suspect. You don't happen to have someone who could pass as a decent photographer, do you?"

"I have an excellent employee whose schedule for the next couple of months opened up just this morning."

"Great. When can he start?"

"She could meet with you tomorrow."

"She?" Of course women could be bodyguards. His mother had a female guard, but it hadn't crossed his mind when he'd thought of the idea.

"Oh, I'm sure Abbie Hastings will be the perfect guard for you and your fiancée."

His daughter? The necktie needed to be loosened again.

two

"I HOPED TO AT LEAST take vacation through Araceli's wedding." Abbie sat across from her father in his office.

"This may give you a new client. I've long felt you have gotten too close to Mandy Crawford to continue to be an effective bodyguard."

It was too easy to let her guard down, especially when she was with the other women she now considered friends. "I understand what you're saying, and I know we need to change Mandy's protection detail, especially when she starts going out with the baby. Do you think Mr. Harmon will at least give me the weekend of the wedding off?"

Jethro chuckled. "Well, you can ask him. He should be here in fifteen minutes."

"Does he come across as spoiled and playboy-ish as he does in the media? I mean, he does go through girlfriends faster than most men go through pizza."

"Abbie—" Her father's stern look reminded her of all the times she'd been in trouble with Alex as a child. "You know it's not for us to judge our clients' lifestyles, and if his girlfriends have been leaving because of these threats, you need to give him some leeway. After all, look at the media mess Daniel got himself into last year. Not everything is as it seems on the surface."

"Well, when he does come, I'll be in my office. I haven't set foot in there for the last month and a half. I can't wait to see what's on my desk."

Her father's laughter followed her down the hall.

Someone had put fresh flowers on the side table. Abbie appreciated the little touch of femininity. Growing up the only girl and sharing hand-me-downs with Alex meant her family tended to forget she enjoyed a few frilly things now and then. One of the perks of guarding Mandy this past year was being able to wear fancy dresses and fashionable business attire to blend in as Mandy's guard. The other perk was getting to know Candace and all the other women of the Art House. Even in her college days, with her criminology major being heavily male, the friendships she'd forged hadn't included many women.

Her desk wasn't piled nearly as high as she expected. Probably because the office took care of most things electronically. There were a few periodicals and catalogs, most of which she tossed in the recycle bin, but she kept the catalog with concealed-carry handbags and other accessories to look at later.

The intercom buzzed, and Marsha's voice came over the loudspeaker. "Your ten o'clock is here. Shall I send him back?"

"I'll come get him."

Abbie studied Mr. Harmon on the monitor for a moment before leaving her office. He looked like he had stepped off one of the covers of his family's fashion and news magazines. She'd once thought Daniel formal, but after the past year, she knew he had a human side, too. She tried to keep an open mind as she rounded the corner to the reception desk. Mr. Harmon stood taller than she'd guessed from the media photos, maybe even a hair taller than Alex's six foot three.

Abbie extended her hand. "Mr. Harmon, nice to meet you."

It took him a beat too long to return the gesture. "Ms. Hastings, I assume."

"Or you can call me Abbie. Come on back to the conference

room, and we can discuss what you need." Abbie led him through the office to a conference room with a clear glass wall facing the cubicles lining the center of the room. Most were vacant as their occupants rarely had need to step inside the office. "Would you like a water or soda?"

At the shake of his head, she closed the conference room door and indicated for him to take a seat. Of course, he took the chair at the head of the table. Abbie bit back her frustration. Her father had told her Mr. Harmon had been surprised he'd recommended a female for the job. It wasn't the first time a client thought she would not be able to be a bodyguard due to her gender. During her three years with the Secret Service, she'd run into gender bias quite often. Abbie took a seat between the table and the window with a view of Lake Michigan, which also gave her a view of the conference room door and outer office.

"Mr. Harmon—"

"Preston, please."

"Okay. Preston. I have been given the notes from yesterday's meeting, the list of former girlfriends and known persons of interest you emailed my father yesterday, as well as the threatening poem Yvette received." She continued at his slight nod. "As you predicted, the only fingerprints we could find belonged to your girlfriend. I reviewed some of her social media and video blog posts, and I agree placing me as a special wedding photographer should work well. I will also have access to Yvette in places the male bodyguard you wanted to hire could not go, such as dress fittings, bridal showers, and the hen party."

Mr. Harmon leaned forward. "I hadn't thought of those things yesterday when I spoke with your father. But you have a good point. You'll pardon me for saying you are not what I expected."

"Do I want to know what you expected?"

Preston smiled, his perfectly straight white teeth probably the result of aligners and veneers. "I've seen your brothers on the job, and I expected you to be more—"

"Muscular?"

"That isn't how I was going to term it. You look so average."

Abbie paused a minute before answering. "My averageness is what allows me to blend in. I assure you, Mr. Harmon—"

"Preston."

"As I was saying, you have seen me on the job on several occasions. However, I normally blend in as much as possible. I can name at least six events in the last five months where we were both in attendance."

Preston's brows furrowed as he studied Abbie. She tried to appear relaxed, but his intense scrutiny unnerved her. "You wore your hair down at Daniel Crawford's New Year's party, didn't you? I noticed you with one of the bodyguards, but I assumed you were trying to flirt with him. Some bodyguards are too irresistible to certain types of women."

"I'm sure my twin will love to hear that one. My goal today is to look, as you say, perfectly 'average.' But I am not. At the moment I am carrying more than one weapon. In hand-to-hand fighting, I have bested my brothers in sparring rounds. Last year I took down a football coach nearly three times my size in a particularly satisfying moment." She knew she sounded a bit snarky, but she didn't appreciate his calling her average. She may not be a six-foot, size-zero model, but at five nine she wasn't out of modeling-height range and had once passed as a model for a job.

"I think you will do quite nicely. I apologize if I offended you. Shall we discuss the details?"

She resisted the urge to toss him out of the room. Instead, she would prove herself to another male chauvinist.

Preston pulled up his calendar on his phone. "This is my Yvette calendar. I'll share it with you. Will the email on your business card work?"

Abbie nodded and pulled out her phone. It beeped, and she opened the calendar.

"I am planning on proposing tomorrow. She is somewhat expecting me to or hinting I should. I have been debating about introducing you before the proposal, but I'd rather not have her reaction staged. If you could be there, perhaps taking a few photos from a distance, you can show her what photos you took when I introduce you as a bridal gift."

"What about your security team? Won't you have someone somewhere nearby? They could get suspicious if I'm taking photos."

"Oh, you are right. I better let them know I hired a photographer. That will be tricky. Simon Dermot will insist on a background check."

Abbie shared his scowl. "I suppose my name will raise eyebrows as well as lead to questions. So I will need to work under a pseudonym. I have a couple: Gale Henderson and Gaileen Harris. Either should pass a basic background check. How in depth do you think they will dig?"

"Considering the threats to my past girlfriends, I would expect them to do a fairly thorough search."

Abbie bit her lip. "Sadly, we are not the FBI or CIA. I doubt my false identities can withstand heavy scrutiny. I think "Gaileen" sounds more like an up-and-coming photographer."

"Do you know if any of Simon's team would recognize you?" Preston twirled his pen, a nervous habit he'd acquired as a boy.

"Considering I've worked the same events as many of them, I'd be surprised if someone didn't recognize me." Abbie wrote a note on the pad in front of her. "Is there anybody you can trust on your security team?"

"I'll have to bring Simon Dermot in on this. He's worked for my father for thirty-five years, and I think he's getting ulcers over the stalker. I trust him. If he signs off on your background check, no one will question it. But how are you going to prevent other people from recognizing you?"

"That is for me to worry about. If you don't have anything else, I'll see you tomorrow at three." Abbie stood and extended her hand again. Preston followed her lead.

He left the office, his hand still slightly paralyzed from the firm handshake he'd received. Abbie Hastings wasn't what he'd envisioned at all, but she might work.

three

THE WIG ITCHED. ABBIE WISHED she'd had time to drive down and peruse Candace's collection. The short-cropped hair with bleached ends not only stuck out in all directions but poked her in the scalp as well. But with an hour before the proposal, she didn't have time to change her appearance. She'd already sent a current photo of Gaileen to Preston to share with Simon Dermot. She'd opted for a subdued, artsy look. The temporary tattoo would be a bit of a pain to keep reapplying in the same spot along her collarbone, but it was better than a nose piercing. The round eyeglasses caused sweat to drip down her nose. She thought about discarding the wig, but the risk of a member of Simon Dermot's security team recognizing her was too high.

She walked around the park again, her earlier texts with Preston indicating he intended to propose on the south side of the fountain. Not the best for three-o'clock lighting. From a bench about fifteen feet away, she could pretend to read while she photographed the happy moment. At twenty till, she spotted two of Simon's team walking the perimeter. They must not be thrilled with this location either—far too much pedestrian access. One guard approached her, paused, then looked at his phone and back at her before walking away. He must've gotten the memo stating she worked for Preston.

The other guard circled the other side of the fountain. He had a familiar swagger to his step. *No.* Of all people, he would recognize her instantly. She had forgotten Dermot Security had hired Patrick. They'd dated briefly in high school, until Abbie's brothers had unceremoniously interrupted their first kiss and put Patrick in a headlock. Over the last few years, they had run into each other at events. On the few occasions they'd spoken, he'd asked if her brothers thought she was old enough to take care of herself yet. She'd made the mistake of mentioning it to Alex. The last time she'd run into Patrick was at the Crawford's New Year's party when he'd passed her in the hallway and made a suggestive comment. Before she could take care of the situation, Alex had gone all He-Man and backed Patrick into a corner. No fists were thrown, only words, the brief altercation ending with Patrick walking away. She doubted her brother had caught the last snide remark: "It's not like you're worth protecting anyway. No man wants a woman who is tougher than he is."

If Patrick worked as one of Preston's regulars, she would need to get Preston to alter the schedule. Thankfully, Patrick took no interest in her, circling the fountain once before heading north. He returned a few minutes later with a floral box under his arm. At the sound of approaching laughter, Patrick set the box on the fountain's edge and retreated into the shadows of the trees on the far side.

Abbie checked her cameras through the monitor on her tablet. She had set up two high-resolution hidden cameras to capture the occasion on video. Her secondhand Canon lay concealed in her half-open backpack, ready for the right moment.

Preston hadn't worn a suit, but the button down with rolled-up sleeves failed to convey the casual tone he had probably been shooting for. Yvette's high heels clicked on the stone walkway as she approached the fountain. Abbie had never understood the point of wearing heels with jeans.

Only snatches of their conversation were audible over the water splashing from the carved statues.

When Preston went to one knee, Abbie pulled out her Canon and started taking stills.

A ring was presented, the stone caught the light, and Yvette made the requisite squeal of delight. Abbie glanced at the video feed. Perfect.

The kiss was Hollywood-film worthy. When it ended, Preston signaled for Abbie to join them.

Yvette pouted. "Pressy, you should have warned me. I didn't get the proposal on video or photos."

"Dear heart, you did. May I introduce your engagement gift? This is Gaileen. She caught it all. For the next month, she will be on hand to document everything."

"You got me my own photographer?" Yvette's squeal outdid the one she'd emitted upon seeing the ring. "Oh, Pressy, you are the best!" This kiss was uncomfortably intimate and ended with Preston pulling away. Abbie photographed the moment.

Preston handed the floral box to Yvette, who, playing to the camera, opened it with a flourish. A tiny piece of Abbie felt sorry for Preston, but then, Yvette fit the trophy bride stereotype. Maybe it was what he wanted.

Abbie got a couple of shots in before Yvette pulled the bouquet out of the box. "Pressy, you should have gotten roses. But these do smell—"

The flowers flew toward the camera as Yvette shrieked. "SPIDERS!"

Both security guards materialized before Yvette's scream ended and she landed on her backside in the fountain. Seeing things were under control, Abbie kept her cover and shot more photos.

Whipping her wet hair out of her face, Yvette flung expletives and water droplets with each splash. Preston involuntarily took a step back. She had never spoken to him like this.

"I hate spiders, you stupid jerk! Where did you get these from? The corner convenience store? One of your budgeting initiatives?" Yvette begrudgingly accepted Patrick's hand and stood, the water streaming off her, her silk blouse clinging to her impossibly shapely form. Onlookers attracted by her shrieks watched the spectacle from behind raised phones. Yvette turned her ire on Abbie. "Stop! Taking! Photographs! If so much as one photo is posted online, I'll sue your spiky hairdo until you're bald!"

Abbie knelt by the flowers and took a few photos until one of Preston's bodyguards tapped her on the shoulder. "She told you to stop."

"I thought you might like a couple of shots as evidence before all the spiders ran away."

Yvette pointed. "See? Spiders. YOU. KNOW. I. HATE. SPIDERS!"

The guard grunted and resumed his position, trying to shield Yvette and Preston from the crowd's view.

Preston pasted on what he hoped resembled an enduring smile. "Dear heart, let's go someplace more private to discuss this."

"There is nothing to discuss. Notes, a black rose, death threats, and now spiders! I don't care what Mama says. You are not worth it. You are a terrible kisser, and I would probably die of boredom on our wedding night! I don't care how many millions or billions you have in the bank. Just look at me!"

Preston tried not to. With mascara running down her face and the rest of her makeup melting under her wilted hair, she was not a pretty sight. And her voice! He had no idea she could reach such shrill notes. His cousin had been right. Again. Yvette wasn't suitable for the job of wife. She lacked a certain depth that he hoped for.

A flash from a phone camera caught her attention, and Yvette whirled. "Lose the camera! Now!"

But her words were useless against the dozen phones aimed in her direction. Yvette turned to Patrick. "Give me your coat!" He shrugged out of his jacket, and she tented herself with it.

"Get me out of here!" she screamed, then stomped off with the bodyguard in tow.

As Preston watched them leave, he knew he should feel something at her rejection. But the words she had thrown at him had extinguished any feelings of warmth he'd held for her. He'd never loved her. Love had little place in marriages like his. An empire could be built with the right woman by your side. Obviously, Yvette was not that woman. The onlookers disbanded with the drama.

Abbie held out the floral box. "I took the liberty of boxing them back up. Some of the spiders are gone, but I believe all of them are of a common household variety, newly hatched."

His other bodyguard took the box from her. "Thank you, miss. Since Mr. Harmon has no further need of your services, his secretary will pay your fee as soon as you hand over the original files you took today to Dermot Security." The guard handed her a card.

"No, give the cards directly to me now. Then there is no need for you to travel across town." Preston held out his hand.

Abbie ejected the card from her Canon and set it in his palm. Her gum snapped as she talked. "Whatevs. Gimme a minute to get the other two cameras."

"Two cameras?"

Abbie sauntered over to a decorative light post, reached up, and removed a small box from the side. She shook her head at his bodyguard, who followed her, every part of her oozing attitude. If Preston hadn't met her in the office yesterday, he would have never guessed she was the same woman. No wonder she claimed to have been in the same room when he hadn't known it. Abbie retrieved another box from a tree, then walked to the bench where her backpack sat. Preston was impressed the bag was still there. One didn't leave bags lying around on benches in Chicago, even in the nicer areas, and expect the bag to not be lifted.

His bodyguard seemed to be arguing with her. Preston approached them.

"No way, dude. Mr. Harmon said to give them to him." She unlocked a retractable cord chaining her backpack to the bench. He recognized the brand. No one would have been able to unzip the bag unless their fingerprint triggered the bio lock.

"Nice bag."

"Ya, too bad I lost this gig. I needed the money for the last payment." Her gum snapped again. Abbie opened the cameras and removed the disks. "Here ya go. Your rent-a-cop wanted them, but I told him they were only for you."

"Thank you, miss," Rats. What name had she said?

"Gaileen Harris. Make sure your accountant spells it right on my check." G-A-I-L-double E-N." She walked off, the second woman in less than ten minutes to do so. Oddly, he felt more of a loss at Abbie's exit.

four

THE ELEVATOR DOORS SWOOSHED OPEN, and Abbie strode past her oldest brother, who waited in the Hastings Security lobby.

"Abbie?" He followed her down the hall to her office.

"Hey, Adam." She took off the glasses, hoping he would not detain her since she was in a hurry to get the rest of the disguise off as well.

"What on earth are you wearing?"

She yanked off her wig, removed the netting cap and bobby pins under it, freeing her hair. Relief. How did Candace wear these things every day? She tossed the wig in the garbage. "Worst wig ever! I was undercover for a job, but I believe it ended prematurely."

"Dad said you had a month-long gig for Preston Harmon." Adam sat down in one of the chairs and put his feet on her desk.

Abbie reached over and knocked his feet off. "Did. Just as well the job ended. Patrick Vonn is one of his bodyguards. I don't think I could go a whole month without punching him."

Adam started out of the chair. "He didn't say anything, did he?"

"Down, brother. He didn't recognize me." Abbie opened an alcohol wipe and started to scrub at the tattoo.

"Well, it took me a moment, squirt."

She aimed the used wipe at his head. It fell short.

"You throw like a girl."

Abbie finished removing the temporary tatt, then used a facial wipe on the heavy eye makeup. "I am a girl who wants to get back into my own clothes, so I'd appreciate it if you went someplace else."

"Fine. Will you be at dinner Sunday? Been missing you with all the time you and Alex have spent in Indiana lately."

"Sure, now get out." She missed mom's cooking too.

After changing, Abbie folded up the clothes and retrieved the wig from the garbage. She might need the outfit again. She pulled out her cell and texted Mandy.

Up for a visit?

— Only if you can smuggle in double-fudge chocolate. Mom is on a health-food kick.

Done.

The office phone rang.

"Abbie Hastings."

"It's Preston. I need your help. Can we meet?"

Five minutes later she texted Mandy again.

Sorry. Work calls. I'll text you when I can come.

— Better bring two pints.

I'll bring three. Tough client.

He half expected her to still be in the disguise she had worn an hour ago or even in business attire. The jeans and layered T-shirts looked comfortable. Too bad her face said she felt otherwise about the meeting. "Thank you so much for meeting me on such short notice."

Abbie led him back to her office, leaving the door open, and handed him a bottled water.

"I didn't expect to see you again today. Did Yvette change her mind?"

"Yes, when I insisted she return the ring. It was one of my grandmother's favorites." Begged, pleaded, cried, and tried every feminine wile she had. By the time she finished he was left disgusted and disturbed. Was this really the type of wife he wanted?

"So I'm back on the job?"

"Not exactly. I had to have security remove her from the guesthouse. She screamed profanities in three languages the entire way." Only after he'd threatened to release the photos Abbie had taken did Yvette return the ring.

Abbie leaned back in her chair. Preston recognized her posture—like father like daughter, and surprisingly intimidating on her, too. "So, if you don't need me to guard your fiancée, what do you need?"

Preston took a sip of water and wondered how she would react. "I need you to be my fiancée."

The chair squeaked as she sat up. "What?"

"I need to catch the stalker. I've wasted the last three years of my life dating woman after woman only to have them scared away. I'll be thirty-five next year, and according to my grandfather, it is time for me to take my place in the family, marry, and carry on the legacy. I can't waste any more time, plus there are only two more women who fit the profile. Not that the profile worked with Yvette. Not sure how we missed that she wanted my money more than me." His thought sounded more reasonable in his mind.

Abbie held up her hand. "Whoa, you are telling me you profile the women you date?"

"Of course. Health history, genetics, personality, financial information."

"You've got to be kidding. Did no one inform you this is the twenty-first century?"

"It's not much more than what the online dating sites do when making a twenty-first-century match." It wasn't like he'd profiled Abbie.

"I'm no expert, but I am witness to several happy relationships between men of your tax bracket and the women they have fallen in love with. Women who probably don't fit your profile."

He reached up to loosen his tie and discovered he wasn't wearing one. "Daniel Crawford got lucky with Mandy."

"What about Kyle Evans? And Sean Cavanagh?" She folded her arms, challenging him.

"The oil baron's grandson? I've heard the marriage is pure folly. Father blames Deah Evans and all her hands-on charity work. Who is Sean Cavanagh?"

"You may have read about him in the news. He inherited a fortune in investments his grandfather didn't realize he owned." She sat back again in the chair.

"Oh, I did read about him—the organ repairman. He knows the Goodings of New York. The newbie doesn't count. He wasn't a billionaire when he fell in love. These are the exception rather than the rule." Preston shook his head. The woman believed in love. He blamed the Hearthfire channel with all its hearts and flowers. Oddly, Abbie's background check showed she'd never dated anyone seriously, but her brothers may be a factor, or maybe she suffered from a broken heart.

She leaned forward and looked him in the eye. "But Sean Cavanagh officially proposed in March—after he inherited."

"I am not sure what your point is or what it has to do with our business. If I am to wed, the stalker must be caught. I've become a joke on social media. '#Prestoned' is trending right now as a euphemism for being dumped."

She covered her mouth briefly before answering. "So me pretending to be your fiancée solves this how? When we catch the stalker, we are going to call off the wedding. And you will have been 'Prestoned' again."

She'd used air quotes. Zero in the sophistication category. This wouldn't work. She didn't even begin to fit the profile in looks or manners. Well, she was tall enough, and she had caught his eye at the New Year's party. But the woman standing across from him barely resembled the lady in the deep -blue evening gown. "Perhaps I've made a mistake." Preston rose from his seat.

Abbie rose as well and beat him to the door. "I am sorry. I should not have laughed at you. Why don't you tell me what you had in mind?"

"We start dating immediately. In a few days, I propose. I already had the Knickerbocker reserved for the wedding as Yvette loved the venue. New announcements can be printed. No one will know our engagement is anything but real. The stalker should have to act fast, which might cause him to make a mistake, and we catch him. End of story."

She moved around the desk and picked up a pad and pen. "Questions first. Are you dating me, Abbie Hastings, or am I taking on a disguise? If so, how much of a wardrobe allowance are you building into the contract?"

"Either way I'll take care of your wardrobe up to $100k. There will be events we need to be seen at, and there won't be time for custom anything other than a wedding dress. I already have the designer on retainer for Yvette. He'll work fast. But I am afraid you will need to meet with him the day after tomorrow to get started. Go get a spa treatment and makeover, too."

"Surely it won't get up to the wedding, will it?" Abbie didn't seem as comfortable in her chair as before.

"I doubt it, but if you use a pseudonym, a fake name will help by invalidating the license. Plus, if the stalker realizes your true profession, he may not buy that our relationship is real."

"I'll have to be Gale Henderson, then, since it's my only other established alias. You will need to let Simon know again." She pulled the end of her sandy-blonde ponytail around and twirled it. "Is Patrick Vonn one of your bodyguards?"

"Yes, why?"

"We have a history. Even if I dye my hair, he may realize who I am."

"I can get him reassigned, perhaps to my cousin, so he won't be around too often. Anything else we need to discuss?"

Abbie walked to the door. "Wait here, and I'll ask my father. I understand it is traditional to ask a father's permission for an engagement, even a fake one."

five

"A MAKEOVER? OF ALL THE nerve! He suggested a spa day and a makeover." Abbie dug another scoop of cherry-chocolate ice cream out of her container.

Mandy stuck her spoon in her pint of double fudge. "Did he offer you a spa day after this is over? That's when you're going to need it."

Candace's voice came over the speaker on Abbie's phone. "Maybe he meant it for your disguise. After all, a new hair color and some colored contacts could be considered a makeover." Car noises littered the background, making it difficult to hear. "Hey, leaving Gary, Indiana, and traffic is picking up. Signing off. Zoe and I will see you two soon. Save us some ice cream!"

Abbie pocketed her phone. "She could be right. I don't think he is being deliberately offensive. Like the first day we met, when he told me I was average."

Mandy held her bulging belly and laughed. "Don't make me laugh. Average? You are anything but average. What planet is he from?"

Not sure how to answer the question, Abbie changed the subject. "I don't want to change my hair so drastically I can't find myself." She pulled the end of her ponytail around to study her hair.

"A raven black like Anne of Green Gables is out?" Mandy adjusted her pillow.

"As I remember, the dye turned her hair green. Double out."

"Take out the hair band. Having your hair down changes your look considerably. You almost always have your hair up or back. With some brown contacts and strawberry highlights and lowlights, you'd get 'I'm sorry, I thought you were…' comments if you ran into someone you knew."

"I could go red. If I was a true ginger, do you think I would know if he had a soul to steal?" Abbie stood in front of Mandy's mirror.

"NO! Laughing! Daniel is ready to get a nurse for me. Mom is already here, and I don't need to be babysat. Stop doing anything that forces my muscles to tighten."

"Sorry, but can laughing start contractions?"

"I don't think so, but I don't like seeing Daniel scared. I have a feeling I might have to pay Alex to keep Daniel out of the delivery room if this keeps up." Mandy rolled her eyes. "Keeping Mom in check is giving her something else to focus on. Especially when she gets going on the birthing rituals of various ancient cultures."

Mandy's phone rang a tune by Savage Garden. Abbie had heard the ring tone enough over the last year. She stepped out while Mandy took her husband's call, and scrolled through her missed texts. There was one from Zoe saying they'd found a traffic jam. Hardly surprising.

Even Preston's texts sounded stuffy.

— **Please contact me. There is a detail we forgot.**

Abbie reread the screen. Nope. He had been thorough.

What did we forget?

— **When will you be moving in?**

When pigs fly. **I wasn't planning to.**

— **But all my other girlfriends have either moved into the west wing or the guesthouse. They all beg to.**

Beg? So not happening.

When this is over, I still need to live with myself. I don't need people assuming something that wasn't. I will stay where I am.

— **Where is that?**

I share a condo with Alex.

— **So there's nothing odd with you living with a guy, just with me? He is my twin!**

— **Not in your current identity.**

Abbie wished she could kick one of Alex's sparring dummies. **Fine. I'll find an apartment or something.**

— **It needs to be nice and have some type of security.**

Seriously? Like I'd take a project on the south end.

Colin Ogilvy owned his building and the one where Daniel and Mandy had their penthouse, plus who knew what. Maybe he could help her get a short-term something. Or she could try Airbnb to find an upscale location. Even at $1k a day, she would make a nice sum on the job. It wasn't like she would blow through the clothing budget in a month.

Let me make some calls.

— **I'll need to approve it.**

She longed to send him an eye-roll emoji. How was she supposed to get through a month-long engagement with this guy? She'd better find the stalker quickly, or she might need to hire a bodyguard to protect Preston from her.

Give me a few hours. I have an idea.

Also, I'll get a different phone. You don't want to have the two versions of me in one text thread.

— **Good idea. I should probably delete this conversation.**

A few snarky comments pulsed at the ends of her fingertips, but she set her phone down and walked to the other side of the room. Why had she agreed to this? Daniel had already paid her a four-month bonus so she could go to Araceli's wedding and spend the entire summer backpacking in Canada. Besides, if Yvette was representative of the type of women Preston customarily dated, the stalker was doing him a favor.

Her phone rang with Candace's ringtone.

"Hey, can you get us in? Mandy forgot to put us on today's visitor's list, and she isn't answering."

"Give me a minute." Abbie disconnected and called downstairs.

The security member was new. "I am sorry, Miss Hastings, but Candace Wilson doesn't match the photos on file. I can't let her in."

"Her file states she has alopecia and is bald. Look at her face, not her hair, and if necessary, scan her fingerprint. It's on file. Or, if you wish, I can come down myself." Taking a bit of her temper out on a guard who didn't know how to read would help.

"Sorry, Miss Hastings. I'll send them up."

"Thank you, and you owe the apology to Miss Wilson."

Candace and Zoe laughed as they exited the penthouse elevator. "What on earth did you say to the poor security guy? He stumbled all over himself apologizing."

The wig of the afternoon reminded Abbie of the '60s hippies with tie-dyed hair. No wonder the guard was suspicious. "Where did you find your wig?"

"It's one of my old ones with some hair extensions. Zoe and I were a bit bored the other day. We brought extensions for each of you, too, for Araceli's hen party."

Mandy called from the sunroom, where she lay on the daybed. "Party in here, please!"

They joined Mandy, and each found a spot as Candace passed around the hair extensions. She gave a tiny set to Mandy as well. "I know you and baby-to-be can't join us in person and your little one won't even be hatched yet, but I couldn't resist making a set for her, too."

"Oh my, these are so precious!" Mandy held up the tiny extensions. Mom claims I was born with a full head of hair. Abbie don't let me forget these when we do the baby's photo shoot." She set them on the low table beside her. "By the way, Daniel said he would be here in an hour, with Colin, for dinner."

Abbie toyed with her phone. "Good. I need to talk to Colin. Preston asked me to move in with him. Which is not happening. So I need to find an upscale apartment I can crash in for a month. I'm hoping there is something in one of his buildings."

Zoe gasped. "He did what? Just what kind of a charade does he think you'll do?"

Abbie opened her phone to the text conversation and passed it around. Candace handed the phone back. "He did offer separate accommodations. But I wouldn't let Alex read this."

"Are you saying he's overprotective?" Abbie pocketed her phone.

"Is Michelangelo Italian?" asked Candace.

Everyone laughed. Mandy held up her hand. "No making me laugh."

Candace knelt in front of the daybed and hugged Mandy. "Sorry, we will try, but you know how impossible this will be."

"I know. Let's work on Abbie's new look. I have so many ideas." Zoe opened her tablet.

Fortunately, the next hour of laughter did not cause any contractions.

Preston was impressed as his driver pulled into the underground garage of one of Chicago's premiere high-rises. Abbie had managed to find a one-month rental in one of Colin Ogilvy's buildings. It proved the axiom about it being who one knew that mattered. The doorman let Preston in and directed him to the elevator for the tenth-floor apartment.

Preston knocked on the door. The woman who answered must be the Realtor. She was on the short side for a model, but her long, strawberry-blonde hair and soft-brown eyes would still get her many jobs. He wondered if she had ever considered the industry. He passed her and went into the furnished living area. The view of the lake was better than most.

"I take it this meets your approval."

That voice. Preston turned to look at the woman again. "Abbie?" He told himself to stop staring, but his eyes wouldn't listen. Had he called her average? The woman in front of him was anything but average.

"Gale Henderson. Glad to meet you." Abbie extended her hand.

It was her. Preston hoped he'd masked his shock. "I didn't recognize you at first. My apologies."

"Well, that gives me hope. I didn't want to go too extreme, but some contacts, hair color, and extensions seems to have worked." She gathered her hair in a ponytail. "And if I need to be the real me, I'm only a ponytail and a pair of jeans away."

Preston cleared his throat. "Sorry for—" No matter what his next words were, he knew they would be wrong, so he stopped talking.

"Sorry for … ?" She raised her eyebrows and waited.

Stupid neckties. He needed to stop wearing them around any of the Hastings. None of his security team ever intimidated him. No one did. Just the Hastings. "Not recognizing you sooner."

Her lips thinned. "Would you like something to drink? Water? Soda? Since you're here, we may as well plot out the next month."

"Water, please." Preston took a seat on the couch.

Abbie brought him a glass. "I forgot I needed to order groceries. By the time I was done with the personal shopper, I wasn't even trying on the clothes she handed me. The last thing I wanted to do was do more shopping." She sat in the chair opposite him. "I should tell you we have extra cameras installed inside the apartment in case your stalker makes it past security."

Preston read the threat between the lines. Anything he did, her father and brothers might see, so no forgetting this was a charade. "I assume Hastings oversees the security for this building?"

She nodded and took a sip of her water. "It has certain advantages. If I use one of the biometric scanners now, my Gale Henderson ID photo shows up. The doorman and all security working this building have been advised I am to be addressed as Gale. Should we plan any get-togethers here with friends or your family? There will not be a problem. We should have something early on to give the stalker a chance to know where I live."

"But would the stalker be able to get past the security?"

"They got past yours."

"Touché."

"Since we need to catch them in the act, security is deceptively lax." Abbie smiled, and for a second, his heart stopped.

One of the reasons he'd chosen her was because he thought he would be able to focus as he felt no attraction to her. Maybe he was as bad as all the men his cousin Felicia was always going on and on about because they would follow anything in a skirt. This particular skirt was soft and flowy and fell below the knees. "Shall we plan for next week?"

Abbie penciled it in on Wednesday on a printed calendar. "I thought it best if the electronic versions of our calendars didn't have some events on them. When we finish, I'll send this over to the office. The wedding is June 28? What else do you have planned?"

Preston turned the calendar to face him. "The proposal should be this weekend. With Monday being Memorial Day, it gives us plenty of time to be seen around town."

Who would believe that? "Today is Friday, and you only got dumped yesterday. I've heard of rebounds, but three days is fast, even for a man—" She paused.

"With my reputation?"

Miss Intimidation looked uncomfortable. Score!

"My reputation for changing girlfriends should help us, then. I am not known for wallowing and waiting for the next woman to come along. I'll claim love at first sight."

Abbie took the calendar back and wrote "proposal" on Monday.

"What are those three days you crossed out?" Preston pointed to the second week of June.

"My friend Araceli is getting married in Boston, to Kyle Evans. I am going, non-negotiable."

"Kyle Evans's wedding? No problem. I'll go too. I am sure I can get an invite if I ask the right person."

"But I need to go as me, Abbie. We can't risk anyone asking questions about why you are there if I am at the wedding as Abbie Hastings. I can't go as Gale Henderson."

"And how will it look if my fiancée up and disappears for three days?"

Abbie rubbed her temples. "I don't want to miss this. Please?"

For a second, he thought she might beg. He got up and walked to the window to distance himself. "I could plan a business meeting in Boston and take you along. Then you could do both, and you would only need to be seen with me at a few things. I could book us a suite at the Ritz."

"Two suites. My back story is I am a want-to-be photographer from an Indiana farm town. I go to church every Sunday, and I still have the purity ring my father gave me. She held up her right hand."

"Where did you get one of those?"

Her cheeks pinked. "Like I said, my father gave it to me. It isn't practical to wear on the job, so few people have ever seen it."

"Two suites."

"Will you be taking any security?"

Preston shrugged. "I generally take a small detail. I'll have to if you have been threatened."

"Can you make sure one of the laxer men on your team gets the assignment? Unless Simon comes, since he will know. I'll need to sneak out of the Ritz and over to the Four Seasons, where the real me is staying. And on Thursday night I don't think the fake me will be able to appear at all. She will have to get some bad lobster or something."

"So the wedding is on Friday?"

Abbie nodded.

"I think that could work. What about the real you's friends?"

"I wasn't asked to be a bridesmaid because of my job as Mandy Crawford's bodyguard. She is no longer going, but all her old roommates are in the bridal party. I don't have as much involvement as the rest of them. The maid of honor and one of the bridesmaids already know I am operating as a split identity this month."

"Wait. I thought we weren't telling anyone."

"No, *you* aren't telling anyone. My father and brothers needed to know as did a couple key employees. I asked Mandy Crawford for advice on a personal shopper and stylist. And since she was asked, and declined, to be one of the bridesmaids for the wedding in Boston, you might surmise at least some of the wedding party knows my business life. None of them could be your stalker anyway. As I was saying, the maid of honor knows and can cover for me. I don't need to be at the rehearsal."

Preston turned his attention back to the calendar. "I guess we fill in the rest with various dates. My mother will want to have an engagement party, and it will drive her crazy if she doesn't have a month to plan. My advice is to stay out of her way and let it happen. She will probably try to be involved in the wedding planning, too, though most of it is prepared, since I booked the venue. You won't mind if she changes the flowers and colors, will you? And she will want to meet your bridesmaids. Who will they be, anyway?"

Abbie shrugged. "Since I don't want to endanger my friends, I wasn't planning on inviting them."

"But you need friends or cousins or something."

"Well, Candace and Zoe are pretty much up to anything, and since they already know, they can play along."

"That reminds me." Preston pulled a card from his pocket. "This is Mateo's card. He is expecting you at eight thirty tomorrow morning for dress measurements and a consult. You'll need to find the bridesmaids dresses off the rack. That will tick off my cousin Felicia, but it can't be helped. Are you sure I can't tell her about you? We have rarely kept secrets from each other."

"No, you can't even tell your parents. Don't worry about the dresses. I am sure I can find something tasteful she will like."

"The less tasteful, the better when it comes to Felicia. She wants to be one of those women who has a dreadful collection of bridesmaid's dresses."

"So, how are we going to meet?"

"Clubbing?" That was where he'd found most of the girlfriends he hadn't found through work.

"I don't drink, remember? You could literally run into me."

"What?"

"Like come through a doorway or turn around too quick in the coffee shop. Or your limo could splash a puddle on me, like in the old movie with the actor my grandma liked."

Preston looked at his watch. "I have an idea. It's perfect. We meet tonight."

six

THE BASIC LITTLE BLACK DRESS emphasized a little too much for her taste. She hadn't realized how short it was during her whirlwind shopping spree. Abbie pulled on the hem as she sat at the table and sipped a second glass of water. Apparently, people didn't come to the upscale restaurant alone. At least she got Preston to drop the book-and-a-rose portion of his plan. After twenty minutes of waiting, she wished she had brought a book, if not to read to at least deflect the increasing number of pitying glances she was receiving from other patrons. The maître d' came by and politely asked if she had heard from the other party. Her cue to leave.

She apologized for taking up a table, collected her clutch purse, and started to stand when a passing customer bumped into her, causing her to stumble. A waiter carrying a tray of filled drink glasses sidestepped to avoid the customer, but the tray slid out of his hands and into Abbie's shoulder, ice and drinks pouring all over her. She fell back against the table. The maître d' and waiter apologized and offered her a towel.

The customer turned to face her, his face full of remorse. "I am so sorry. I believe this is my fault. I bumped into the waiter."

The maître d' turned his attention to Preston. "Mr. Harmon, it is not your fault at all."

"But it is. I wasn't paying attention as I was looking at my phone. Walking and texting causes accidents."

Abbie straightened and cleaned herself off the best she could, glad Preston had insisted on the black dress. The lighter color she had favored would have become translucent with this much liquid. An ice cube slid down the inside of the dress, and she shivered.

"You must be freezing." Preston slipped out of his suit coat and draped it around her shoulders. "Where is your dinner partner?"

Abbie felt her cheeks burn—the only warm spot on her.

"The lady's partner failed to show. She's leaving," volunteered the maître d'.

"So you didn't even get to try their signature dessert? That is a shame. Allow me to take you to change, then I will bring you back."

Abbie shook her head and turned to the maître d'. "If you could hail a cab, please."

Preston stepped forward. "My driver will be here any moment. And if you are concerned about leaving with a stranger, half of the patrons can probably identify me."

"I recognize you, Mr. Harmon—"

"Preston, please."

Another piece of ice started to melt. "Thank you for your kind offer, but I think I should just leave."

"How about I take you to your destination and we return and have dinner on Monday? I can't imagine the agony of sitting here waiting for your date and watching all the incredible food pass by. Admit it. You have seen at least three things you are dying to try."

Abbie couldn't help it. She smiled.

"There. Give me a chance. A dozen witnesses are seeing us leave together, and I think a few have even taken photos. If half of Chicago knowing doesn't ensure you get safely home, nothing will." He gave her a half grin.

A puddle of cola mixed with lemonade and who knew what else started to collect in her shoe. "Thank you for your offer. I accept a ride home."

The maître d' turned to Preston. "Shall I make a reservation at seven on Monday?"

"Please do." He agreed without her approval.

Preston placed his hand on her lower back and escorted her to the door.

As soon as his car came into view, Abbie stopped. "I can't sit in there! I'll ruin the leather."

"No worries. My driver covered the seat, although I admit I didn't expect you to get quite so doused."

Abbie sniffed. "It smells more like I am soused."

The driver opened the door. Preston entered first, and the driver helped her in. The seat was covered with several towels, probably Egyptian cotton, and she buried her face in one Preston handed her. When she pulled the towel away, she caught him appraising her.

She checked to make sure the privacy window was up before speaking. "You could have given me a few more details, like warning me to wear waterproof mascara. *Or a wet suit.*"

"The minute details would have spoiled your reaction. And it was priceless, even for me." He gave her the half grin again.

Abbie dabbed at her hair. "I will admit you did manage a memorable first meeting."

"I'll bet you a new dress a photo is posted and tagged to my account at least three times before we even get to your apartment." Preston gave her a genuine smile. The smile surprised her—not the smile itself but that she was starting to tell which ones were real and which ones weren't.

"Well, considering you bought this one, I don't think it's much of a bet."

"Still, I owe you a new one. This time I'll find a dress that suits you better. A woman should be comfortable in her clothes. Even before I ruined the dress, you were not."

She set the towel in her lap. "How did you know?"

"You must have tugged on your hem a hundred times this evening."

"You watched me?"

"Of course. I had to have a reason to be in the restaurant and to run into you. I met a friend in the bar. We could see you quite well. He did comment on the poor stood-up woman and wondered if he should go pretend to be the missing date. I discouraged him, you're welcome."

The driver pulled up to the curb, but Preston made no move to open the door or let her out.

"Shall we do something else tonight?"

"No, if Monday weren't planned, this would be the point you'd ask for my number and then spend all weekend texting me to convince me I should go to dinner with you on Monday."

His eyes grew wide. "You didn't agree in the restaurant, did you?"

When the driver opened the door, Preston got out and extended his hand. "I hope the rest of your night goes well, Gale." He squeezed her fingertips before letting go of her hand.

Abbie was in the lobby before she realized she was still wearing his coat. She turned, but the car had driven off.

"Something wrong, Miss Henderson?" asked the doorman.

"He forgot his coat."

The doorman shook his head. "He didn't forget it. He planned it, but don't worry. He'll be back tomorrow."

"How do—" She shook her head. "Never mind. Good night." Abbie headed for the elevator.

"I thought you would be out later."

The sound of his cousin's voice startled him. Knowing she would be curled up with a book reading, he looked into the corners of the room. Preston had hoped to avoid conversations for the rest of the evening. "Felicia, what are you doing here? I thought you were in Milan for the week."

"I came to borrow something out of Auntie's library." The voice came from near the window. She held up a book, but he was too far away to see the title. "Or I came back a day early in case you needed a shoulder to cry on after Yvette. The new hashtag isn't fair. You really should go public about the stalker. This dating and being dumped isn't good for your reputation."

A book wasn't her most original excuse for being in his parents' mansion, but with Mum and Dad in the south of France for the month, it was probably the best she could do. Glad you found something to read. He started up the stairway leading to his rooms. It would be easier to tell Felicia nothing rather than any half-truths.

The click of heels followed him across the marble floor. "I'd ask where your jacket is, but I can guess. I suppose you have an excuse to see her tomorrow since she obviously didn't ask you to stay. I must say you work fast. Get dumped on Thursday and then dumping drinks on the next woman you see. I wonder how you planned that. My guess is you watched her from the bar and plotted." She gave him a knowing smile. He would need to be careful. His cousin knew him too well. "There are two versions of video and several stills. She isn't quite your type, but not bad for a rebound romance."

Preston paused before the first stair. Felicia stood only five foot five in heels, and an extra eight inches to his height would make for an awkward conversation. "It was an accident."

"I don't think so." She pulled out her phone. "I've seen several photos and a video. She looks outraged, and she refused you initially. But you look smug—the way you do when a negotiation goes your way?"

"Smug?"

"Don't worry. I doubt anyone who doesn't know you well will

41

see it. There's a certain slant to your eyes."

"I should have never taught you poker."

She refused to let him turn the conversation. "I'm right. You are plotting your next move. I bet you didn't expect her to ignore your presence. But what I want to know is if the posts are true that she never said yes to the date you tried to set up on the spot?"

"So this is why you came to wait for me? To get the firsthand dirt?"

Felicia turned her face into the pout she'd practiced since her third birthday when she hadn't gotten a real yacht. "The only fun in this family is knowing the truth behind the rumors."

"Yes, she is pretty, and yes, the fact she didn't jump at the chance to dine with me on Monday or to further our acquaintance on the ride to her apartment does make me curious. And you are correct that the jacket gives me a reason to see her again. Although I wouldn't be surprised if a dry cleaner delivers it in the morning. I've never met a woman less interested in me in my life." The last part was definitely true.

"Oh, the poor thing."

"What do you mean?"

Felicia twirled her hair and tilted her head. "She became a challenge to you. The one girl in the greater Chicago area who didn't succumb to your charms or your pocketbook. She must have really liked whomever she was waiting for. Instead, she is going to be stuck with you."

Preston shook his head. "For not being there, you sure know a lot."

"According to one post, she sat there for nearly a half hour, growing more despondent and nervous as her dinner partner didn't show. One woman speculated she was waiting for a blind date, a first meeting. But since she didn't have a book or a flower, she wasn't sure. But then again, one must have reservations at least a week or two in advance there. So she wouldn't have needed a prop to be identified. The scum who stood her up—" Felicia spat out the last part. The last few years had soured her on dating. More often than not, her dates would let it slip that they were more intrigued by the family name than her. The fact she wasn't born a Harmon befuddled a few who wondered if she would inherit. "She is better off without the jerk anyway, but I doubt she deserves you on the rebound, either."

Preston sighed. "She probably deserves better. Now, If you don't mind, I do want to take a couple aspirin and go to bed. As you pointed out, it has been a rather difficult week."

"For what it's worth, I didn't think Yvette was right for you from the first. She couldn't carry on a conversation on any topic outside the current fashion trends. She may have looked good on your arm, but there is more to both of our mothers than just being eye candy. Your mom leapt on the idea of web magazines when most people were saying 'Worldwide what?' And mine has done much in the political arena. You need someone who can do that for you."

"I agree. But as you have learned, it's a jungle out there, and I am not sure there is someone out there like our moms for me."

"That's my line."

He yawned. "Good night. Stay and read if you want." He bent down and hugged his cousin. Preston didn't look back as he headed for his suite. Although the house was technically his father's, he saw no reason to live elsewhere as his parents spent less than forty days a year at the primary residence. He was hardly the stereotypical son who hadn't left the nest. As soon as he married, the house would be his to use as he wished. His parents had had the transfer documents drafted at the time of his first engagement.

He checked the security logs. Other than Felicia, only staff had been in the house today. Yvette had been escorted to and from the guesthouse to collect some items she claimed to have left behind. The security officer had noted the items consisted of a coffee mug and T-shirt from a fun run wadded up under the sink. She would not be allowed back again. He sent a text to

Gale Henderson's phone.

Goodnight. Hope you sleep well. If you take the dress and my jacket down to the doorman in the morning, I'll have my dry-cleaner take care of them.

He only had to wait a moment before the answering text came.

— Don't worry. I already sent out your coat. It will be delivered to your office at Harmon Towers.

What about the dress?

— I don't know that it should be saved.

But every woman should have a little black dress.

— Maybe. Thank you for the ride.

Good night.

Supposed to be easy. What if someone looked at one of their phones? Abbie insisted everything appeared authentic. Perhaps he should have inquired what authentic looked like to her. He shouldn't have to work harder for her attention than he did other women's.

seven

"I DON'T LIKE IT. Do you know how dangerous this type of job is?" Alex paced her apartment.

"I don't consider spider-covered flowers or notes left on a bed dangerous." Abbie opened the third of the three dress boxes delivered that morning. Preston had good taste, and all the dresses he'd sent over were better than the black dress she had happily discarded. The first two skimmed the top of her knees. She held the third dress up to see that it fell an inch below her knee, a length she much preferred as too many football games played with her brothers had left her with more than one scar on her knees.

"Not that kind of danger." Alex pointed at the dress. "That kind of danger. He's already figured out your style. You can't fake this type of relationship without some of your own emotions getting involved."

"You've been listening to Adam." She set the longer dress aside to try on. The September job had messed with his head. "Don't worry. I don't have a crush on him or anything. Preston is stuck on image. I think he was surprised when I didn't drool all over him last night in the restaurant. Like every woman should fall for his hazel eyes, athletic build, and pocketbook."

Alex raised an eyebrow. "Hazel? See? I told you undercover work is dangerous."

"Face it. Even you knew that detail." Abbie partially shut the bedroom door so she could change but still talk. The unmistakable thump of Alex leaning back against the wall outside her door reassured her. They had talked like this ever since they were five and their mother had explained how Abbie needed privacy.

"Yes, I knew he had hazel eyes from the reporters. Dazzling hazel, I believe, but that is not the point."

Abbie twirled in front of the mirror. She was in love with a dress. Her mother would never believe it. Mom still pictured Abbie as a tomboy, not a lace type of girl. "The point is, you are now taking your overprotectiveness into my job. You will always be my number-one twin. But someday we will have other people in our lives. Use this job as your practice time to loosen your ties with me a little."

"Ditto for you, sis. Have I ever gone out on a date that was good enough for you?"

"Don't go there. I let you get married in the first grade. And I have never threatened any of your dates. You need to stop expecting women to understand you the way I do."

She emerged from the bedroom, satisfied when Alex crossed his arms and scowled. If it were up to him, she would wear a potato sack.

"How does he even know your size?"

"I don't know. I had a consultation with the wedding-dress designer this morning. I think the only thing he didn't measure was my little toe. I'm sure Preston could have found out my size from him. Fortunately, Mateo, the designer, had a dress started. It's the dress I'd want if I really got married. I wonder if Preston will let me keep the gown for someday."

"Abbs, you are talking weddings. Real ones. What if you don't catch the stalker in the next few weeks? Have you thought about that? You'll be walking down the aisle like some actress." Alex flopped onto the couch.

"And you will be helpless to do anything."

"Pretty much."

"Don't worry, I doubt it will get that far. But I should let you know he is proposing Monday night. I am not sure where or when. I asked him to keep the details a surprise, but after last night, I am not sure it's wise."

"Are you telling me there will be some PDA?"

Abbie nodded. "A proposal without a display of affection would be unbelievable."

"I don't like it, Abbs. I don't like it at all."

"I know, but the stalker needs to be found. Preston isn't my favorite person in the world, but he isn't half bad in the ten seconds when he forgets to be a stuck-up suit or trust-fund kid. And even if I think he is going about choosing a wife wrong, he still should be able to have a chance."

Confusion clouded Alex's face. "A chance for what?"

"To find his happily ever after. Which he can't do as long as the stalker is out there." Abbie returned to her room to change into something else.

Walking along the Lakefront trail eating an ice cream cone wasn't on Preston's list of first-date ideas. But then, Abbie wasn't as high maintenance as most of his former girlfriends. The Saturday-afternoon outing included watching a Little League game—a far cry from watching the game from the private box at Wrigley Field, but more fun.

Abbie claimed not to know kids on either team, but she did cheer for the blue team more often. Preston had played some sports at the boarding school, but he never participated in the type of team sports where parents cheered for their kids. Mum and Dad did manage to show up for the annual polo game against their rival school. Abbie had grown up in a different world, one where parents didn't have to keep guard against crazies in search of kidnapping money or where the nanny knew more about first words and first steps than the mother did.

Abbie broke into his thoughts. "It is perfect kite-flying weather. Have you ever flown a kite?"

"Of course I have." In the privacy of his backyard.

"Don't look so insulted. You hadn't bought a dog from a stand either. And ketchup? You are a disgrace to your city." Her mellow, vibrant laugh caused a longing for something he didn't know existed.

"I happen to like ketchup." Preston thought the vendor had called him a tourist under his breath.

When she laughed again and touched his arm, he had to remind himself she only acted the part. But the warmth in her touch was very real. No woman had touched him that way since his sophomore year at Harvard. Brita had come from Sweden and hadn't realized who he was when they'd started their relationship. The three weeks before she figured out his net worth comprised the most real relationship he'd ever had. Even screening potential girlfriends hadn't helped him find that elusive connection. "Do you want to fly kites?"

"Cricket Hill has the best kite flying. A few weeks ago they held a kite festival there. It will be perfect if we can find kites."

Preston pulled out his phone and asked the search engine where to buy a kite. "There's a store a couple miles from here. Do you want my driver to get them, or go pick one out?"

Abbie rolled her eyes. "You have to pick out your own kite. Unless you are making it. Making one is the best."

"You've made kites?"

"Mom's a master. She builds these box kites that make everyone else stop and look."

Preston finished his cone and took her hand. There were callouses. Abbie's hands didn't have the spongy, overlotioned feel of Yvette's or anyone else's he'd dated. Didn't she worry about her skin? He added lotion to his list of possible gifts. Felicia could help him find a scent fitting for Abbie.

As for the rest of the gifts, he doubted some of his standards would work. A diamond necklace or tennis bracelet? He had a hard time picturing her wearing either.

They found the shop. It didn't take long before Abbie chose a butterfly kite costing less than twenty dollars. Preston showed her a kite ten times the price.

"No, that is a stunt kite for more experienced fliers. There is no point in wasting money on more than we need. The butterfly is more than enough. One of the twelve-dollar triangle kites would work, but I figured you could afford to spoil me a little bit."

Preston shook his head. He had no reference for dealing with her.

He paid for the kite.

At the end of their date, he realized he'd spent less than fifty dollars for an entire day of fun. Grandmother's oft-repeated statement that money didn't buy happiness floated through his memory.

eight

THE NEW BLACK DRESS MADE her want to twirl like a three-year-old. Abbie propped her phone on the counter and twirled so Mandy could see it over the video conference.

"Oh, so sexy modest! If I didn't look like a whale, I would steal it from your closet. You rock the modern-princess look."

"And I can carry under it. The last one left no place for a gun." Abbie put her hand on her hip, as close to the gun in her thigh holster as she was going to get.

"Don't go ruining the picture. I mean, I know you always carry, but I'd rather not think of you in a dress with a gun." Mandy made a face.

"Remember, this whole weekend is part of my job as body-guard—only at the moment I am guarding myself."

"Anything odd happen yet?"

"A black rose showed up in an unmarked floral box at the door-man's desk, with a note saying I should stay away from Preston. A service delivered it, but so far no new leads. Dad has the PI guys running down Preston's lists of exes. A couple are promising. One woman he dated about five years ago posted a blog about how he ruined her life, but they can't find her."

Candace's face joined Mandy's on the screen. "Love the dress. He picked it out?"

"I haven't asked. I'm sure he has people for that sort of thing." Abbie bent to adjust the straps on her low heels. She would need to return the pairs of high heels she'd purchased as she couldn't run in them, leaving her to wonder how actresses did it in '80s detective shows. "He probably hasn't even seen it. Do you think I need a jacket or something with it? It's going to be below sixty degrees by eleven."

"I say no. Then he can offer you his coat," said Candace.

Mandy took the phone from Candace. "I have something you can borrow. I hear Alex in the other room with Daniel. I think he is leaving. He could bring it over." She turned from the phone and gave Candace directions about where to find a particular shawl in her closet.

"Preston is supposed to be here in twenty, so Alex will need to hurry." She didn't want to face her twin again. Sunday, all her brothers had ganged up on her at dinner, reminding her not to make Adam's mistake. The fact that she'd only stayed for two hours didn't help. Dad and Andrew were her only supporters. Mom claimed she had no opinion. She had been almost glad to need to leave early to meet Preston for the evening.

"It's two buildings over. He'll make it." Mandy looked satisfied. Abbie was willing to put up with a little extra primping if it gave her friend some relief from the boredom of bed rest.

"What are you doing tonight, another movie?"

"No, I am going to play 'track Preston' on social media. I got good at tracking billionaires last year. I can't wait to see the proposal. After he sees you in that dress, I bet you two chick flicks and a pound of chocolates he wishes he was proposing for real."

Abbie checked her hair in the mirror. The curling rod had done its job. She hadn't been this nervous for a date since prom, which was ridiculous. Other than the family dinner, she'd spent the entire weekend with Preston, including a church service. More than once it became apparent that her lifestyle puzzled him. But ditto for her. He didn't even know how to order a proper hot dog!

And who looked at $600 kites if they were not a serious hobbyist? "If we were really dating, there wouldn't be a date today. He is cute enough but has a silver spoon fused to his backbone. He is nothing like Daniel. I have the feeling he has never seen how the 99 percent live."

"Too bad you didn't meet him when you were seven. You could have set him straight." Mandy smiled like she did whenever she was thinking of her husband. It was cute how she still got all sappy-eyed.

The bell buzzed. "That must be Alex. Talk later."

Her brother handed her the silk shawl. "Not much defense against a cold breeze. I still don't like you taking Harmon's job. Candace and Mandy are acting like you never date and this is real."

"We went over this on Saturday and yesterday. I know the difference." Abbie played with the shawl in the mirror. The little rose-buds added color to the ensemble. Wearing black to be engaged in reminded her of some sort of odd funeral.

"I don't see why you had to live here."

"I miss you too. In fact, I put your favorite protein drink in my grocery order by mistake. There's one waiting in the fridge."

A knock sounded. Abbie shooed her brother into the kitchen and signaled for him to stay.

He'd known the dress was perfect for her. It was worth getting Mateo peeved at him for being woken up before noon and every extra dollar the designer required. Preston handed over the single red rose he brought, going for a simpler tone than his usual style. "I hope this rose is more acceptable than the one delivered this morning."

Abbie brought the flower to her nose. "Come in while I see if I can find a vase." Cupboards banged, and water ran in the sink. She returned carrying a soda bottle. The rose leaned to one side.

"Furnished apartment didn't include a bud vase. It was this or a drinking glass."

"Remind me to buy you a vase."

A slight pink blush added color to her cheeks. It wasn't the first time she blushed this weekend, and he found he enjoyed it. Most of the women he dated rarely blushed, although he suspected the Russian model could on command.

"You don't need to buy me a vase or even bring me roses. But thank you."

A tall, broad-shouldered man Preston didn't recognize walked out of the kitchen carrying a drink. "Abbs, do you want me to leave these here or take them all with me?"

She wouldn't move into the guesthouse, but she would keep food for some guy in her fridge? Abbie glared at the man for a moment before turning back to Preston. "My twin, Mr. Alexander."

The handshake was too firm to be friendly. "Mr. Alexander. Nice to meet you."

Abbie gave her brother a warning glare. "Alex, will you lock up when you leave? I don't think I need a bodyguard from Hastings following me out of the building when one of Simon Dermot's men is likely to be the driver."

Alex folded his arms and leaned against the wall. "Sure, sis." He locked eyes with Preston. "Take care of her." If this was the type of reception Abbie's male friends usually received, it was no wonder she was still single. One mystery solved. Poor Abbie. Dating must be a nightmare with a brother who guarded her so closely.

They crossed the hall to the elevator.

"Sorry."

"Does he do that often?"

The elevator door opened, and they stepped in.

"He isn't very keen on me taking this particular job. One of the joys of four brothers is their ability to scare off undedicated dates. The other is if we lose the basketball game, it always gets blamed on me since I'm the short one."

"So why Mr. Alexander and not Hastings?"

"It is easier around the office to have Mr. Adam, Mr. Alan, Mr. Alexander, and Mr. Andrew than have five Mr. Hastings."

"Alex doesn't approve of this job?"

"None of my brothers do. Adam was in a similar situation a couple of years ago when the lines got blurry and he was not himself for a while after."

The elevator opened to the lobby, and Preston escorted Abbie to the waiting car. Being an only child, he envied the camaraderie Abbie shared with her brothers. Felicia was only a cousin, and he had never felt protective of her. He felt concern, but he would never get involved in her personal life.

The conversation at the restaurant lagged as Abbie made the switch into Gale mode. Interesting he hadn't noticed the difference before. Gale's personality was softer than the bodyguard's. Which one was real, or were both a show?

nine

THE SAME MAÎTRE D' LED them to the table where she'd spent a half hour sipping water only three days ago. The restaurant was packed. Abbie wondered how many of the patrons were here because of Preston's unanswered invitation Friday night.

Preston didn't bother looking at the wine list when he ordered. Abbie stopped the waiter. "Excuse me. May I have Perrier?"

The waiter nodded and left. Preston raised a brow. "Perrier?"

"I don't drink on the job."

"But if a job requires it?"

The waiter returned and poured their drinks. Abbie sipped her water. "Never happened. I don't drink off the job either. Even if my father hadn't taught us drinking was unhealthy, I've seen far too much in my line of work to doubt him."

Preston paused and studied his glass. "Well, I have made it a habit not to drink if the company I'm keeping doesn't." He called the waiter over and exchanged his drink.

"I should have told you sooner. It just didn't come up."

"Don't be. At least we will have witnesses that I am not inebriated."

By the end of the first course, Abbie realized most of the customers were more interested in her food than she was. The conversation turned to favorite movies and actors.

"Audrey Hepburn?"

Abbie thought for a moment. "My three favorites again?" At his nod, she continued. "*My Fair Lady*, although I think it's a shame she didn't do the singing, *Charade*, and *How to Steal a Million*."

"Not *Breakfast at Tiffany's*? I thought that was everyone's favorite."

"Not mine. Okay, Cary Grant."

"Seriously, he is in chick flicks."

"Like *Gunga Din* and *North by Northwest*?"

Preston laughed. "I've never seen either."

"How have you gotten through life without seeing *North by Northwest*?"

Preston shrugged. "Mum hated Hitchcock movies. *Psycho* gave her nightmares, and she refused to see any others, so I never saw it."

"Then I suggest we either find a film festival or make one ourselves."

"That can be arranged."

"I'm sure it can. Let me guess. You have a private theater with a full-sized screen in that mansion of yours."

"Nope. But my uncle does. Ours is a quarter of the size. We can find a few friends and have a party anytime you want."

Abbie finished her main course. "I'll hold you to that one."

The waiter set a covered dessert tray on the table and left.

Even though she knew the proposal was coming and the relationship wasn't real, butterflies still invaded her stomach. After all, it might be the only proposal she ever got.

"*Third time's the charm.*" The old axiom echoed in his brain. Or "*Three strikes and you're out.*" At least Abbie wouldn't be saying yes because she meant it. And he wasn't actually proposing, so it wasn't really the third time. More like 2.5.

He lifted the cover of the little black box. The collective intake of breath from the surrounding tables drowned out Abbie's reaction. When Preston slid out of his chair on to his knee, applause erupted before he could open his mouth.

Abbie covered her mouth, her eyes wide, as Preston slipped the ring on her finger and kissed it before standing and offering his hand to assist her to rise as well.

Over the years, Preston had come to believe he was a relatively good kisser. He had kissed women in front of the camera before, but he had never kissed anyone he was paying to kiss him. Before Abbie's eyes closed, he realized her smile wasn't in them. He kept the kiss only long enough to satisfy onlookers before pulling back.

He whispered in her ear. "Dessert here or to go?"

"Here is fine." She sat back down, and he signaled to the waiter.

He usually enjoyed the chef's chocolate creations, but tonight's dessert could have been from a fast-food chain and he wouldn't have been able to tell. He hoped Abbie enjoyed hers more. He held her hand across the table more to reassure her that everything was going to be all right than anything else.

When his driver closed the door, he let out a sigh. "We need to talk."

Abbie pointed to the driver and mouthed "Later." He held her hand, and they sat together in the center of the seat for the duration of the drive.

When the car pulled up to the curb, Preston gave Abbie's hand a caress. "May I walk you up?"

"Please."

Another couple entered the elevator after them. So much for talking.

Abbie looked up at him and gave him a half smile. "Come inside for a minute."

Still holding her hand, he followed her off the elevator.

Once they were inside the apartment, she entered a code in the alarm pad, then another code. "Just so you know, all the cameras are still working, but I have turned off the audio. My brothers don't need to hear everything we say. Give me a moment to make sure Alex left. Do you want something to drink?"

Knowing she didn't have any of his usual after-date drinks, he declined and took a seat on the couch facing the window.

Abbie returned with two glasses of water. "Something happened tonight. What did I do wrong?"

"Nothing. You didn't do anything wrong. I did."

Abbie sank into the seat next to him. "What do you mean?"

Preston stood and began to pace the room. "I shouldn't have put you in that position ... I'm not saying this well. It was the kiss. I realized I paid you to kiss me. And that is not who I am. It isn't who you are. You are an honorable woman, and I treated you—" He leaned against the window frame and looked out at the lake.

Abbie came to stand at the opposite side of the frame. "Preston, when I took this job, I knew being a fake fiancée involved a few public kisses. You didn't take advantage of that tonight. You kept the kiss short and sweet. You didn't push or take advantage."

He turned to face her. "But it isn't right."

She touched his arm. "Come sit down." She waited until he joined her. "I know this is weird, but I respect you for how you feel about this. I didn't think you had it in you. I know that sounds rude, and it is. After our first meeting, I didn't think you could, um, ... well, care." She gave the funny little smile he'd seen a few times over the weekend. He had yet to decipher its meaning but hoped he would before long.

"I probably deserve that. So, where do we go from here?"

"Do you want to call this off? We can wait until you have a real girlfriend and work from there."

Preston gulped down most of his water. "We have come this far, and—"

"You don't need another failed relationship, especially within a week of the last one."

"That too. But I just want this to be over." He began to pace.

Abbie blocked his path. "So we continue as planned. You hired me to find the stalker, and the plan was to pose as your fiancée. And considering you managed to convince the entire restaurant I am engaged without even proposing, I'd say we are off to a good start."

"I didn't propose, did I? And you didn't say yes."

"Nope. Now for my question." She held up her left hand. "Is this a family heirloom, and how much is it worth?"

"It was my grandmother's, and I am not telling you, because you might faint."

"Well, I'm glad I have a safe in the apartment, and I am carrying."

Preston sat up. "You are carrying? Where?"

"If you were my real fiancé, I'd tell you."

"Not show me?"

Abbie smiled. "Nope, you'd have to be my husband to see."

Preston laughed. "Well, then, I guess that's my cue to go. Lunch tomorrow?"

"The more often we are seen together, the faster the stalker will act." Abbie walked him to the door.

"If I give you a kiss on the cheek as a friend, will your brothers be after me?"

"Probably." She grabbed his lapels and went up on her toes and kissed his cheek. "But they won't go after me. Thanks for the best nonproposal I have ever had."

Preston took an empty elevator down to the lobby, then took out his phone to call his driver.

He had four missed texts. Yvette, Felicia, Dad, and Mum. He wondered how long he could go before they started calling.

ten

CANDACE WORE THE SAME WIG she had to Mandy's wedding—a good thing as the bridesmaid's dress she held up would have clashed with anything else.

"That is beyond hideous." Zoe held up a silky pink dress.

"Well, yours looks like you are trying to seduce the best man." Felicia managed to find a ruffled peach gown that looked like it had run away from the '70s.

Abbie hadn't made up her mind about Preston's cousin, but he had been right. She did seem to want to find the hideous gowns. Their meeting yesterday afternoon at the Kickerbocker to go over reception menus with Preston hadn't been awkward per se, but she did get the idea that Felicia didn't entirely approve of her either.

"No, Zoe, not the strapless one, my figure will never support it." Candace turned Zoe back to the rack before Abbie could see what she was carrying.

"I know—why don't I pick a color and you chose your favorite two dresses in that color, then you can mix and match it? That way Felicia can be as atrocious as she wants, Candace can have sleeves, and Zoe can have whatever. No one would ever wear the dresses after the event. What about burgundy or something complementary? With an evening wedding, I think that is better than the pale-rose color."

Candace found her dress first, a lace bodice with sleeves over a trumpet skirt. She could wear it at the Crawford's next New Year's party.

If someone wanted to seduce the best man, any of the dresses Felicia chose would work. The off-the-shoulder draped ruffle sleeves and thigh-high slit on her final choice left little to the imagination. Abbie wondered who the groom's men were.

Zoe couldn't decide between a shimmery silver strapless and a sleek crepe dress with a half Obi-style bow.

"I realize the silver complements the other two dresses, but the shimmery fabric will draw people's eyes away from the bride." Felicia voted against the dress. Abbie fought not to raise her eyebrows, considering Felicia's own choice.

Shoes, necklaces, and handbags came next. Abbie hoped at least some of it could be returned, but she had the feeling Preston wouldn't care about spending $5k on three nonexistent brides-maids. She was still well within her clothing budget. She joined them in the trying on of shoes.

Felicia handed her a pair of spiky heels. "You need to be taller for the photos."

Abbie held up a one-inch satin wedge. "This pair is perfect. I don't have to worry about tripping down the aisle, and I don't want to tower over my bridesmaids."

Just when Abbie thought the morning would never end, they were done and the women piled into the service car and headed to Abbie's for a light lunch.

Abbie unlocked the door to her apartment and put her arm up, barring the others's entry. "Stop." She set the bag containing her new shoes down and pulled some tissue paper out of the box, then used the paper to pick up the paper lying inside the door.

Roses are red,

Violets are blue.

If you want to be dead,

Say "I do."

"Preston warned me about the stalker when I got a black rose on Monday. Don't touch it. I need to text him."

Felicia took a step back toward the elevator. "Is it safe to go in the apartment?"

If Preston's cousin wasn't here, she would clear the apartment herself. She couldn't reveal how wired the place was either. "Let's shut the door and get some of the building's security men to check it out." Instead of calling downstairs, she called Alan. In moments, two security guards emerged from the stairwell. She shot off a quick text to Preston.

Stalker struck, left poem.

Preston read the text a second time before calling Abbie.

"Hi, Preston. We finished up with building security. It was just a poem. I thought Felicia was going to faint for a moment, but she is fine now. The chocolate dessert fixed everything."

"I'll remember that for future reference. Do you need any extra chocolate?"

"No, I am doing well."

He heard voices in the background, so he couldn't ask anything she couldn't answer as Gale. "How did dress shopping go?"

"Do you want to know now or when you get the bill?"

Preston laughed. "Knowing you, it's still ten times less than I expect but more than you ever dreamed. I take it the festivities are continuing?" He longed to ask the questions she couldn't answer.

"We barely sat down to lunch."

"Come to dinner with me tonight?"

"I'd love to. I think I had better get back in there now. They sound like they are planning the movie party and adding a few surprises. Bye, Preston."

The line disconnected. Nothing in Abbie's voice betrayed any worry, so Preston tried not to worry either.

His assistant buzzed.

"Your two o'clock is here."

"Thanks, send them in."

"No fingerprints, DNA, fibers?"

Adam sat back in his chair. "Sorry, Abbs. Other than lacking in originality, the note gave us nothing. The only interesting piece is the stalker used the identical letters from copies of the magazines he used in the first note."

"How did he get the paper under my door without the cameras picking him up?" Abbie started to slouch and thought better of it. Her blouse was sure to wrinkle.

"At 10:13, a private delivery man walks by with several packages, including a long tube. Someone passes him, and the tube seems to bump the camera. Changing the angle enough to leave your door in a dead spot."

"Rather convenient."

"Yes, but the man was the carrier the architect two doors down regularly uses. All the packages were from his agency."

"Could the person who bumped the deliveryman have moved the camera with something else?"

"Possibly. Then three minutes later your motion detector picks up movement near the door and the camera catches the paper on the floor." Adam rolled the video again.

"Go back to the hallway view. Do you see the shadow?"

Adam moved to a different view. "The camera at the end of the hall shows no one there, but it shows a shadow too."

"Looks like the stalker is wearing one of those full-body suits like stagehands wear in the theater but instead of black, it's a light gray. If the camera wasn't HD the person could be dismissed as a blip on the screen." Abbie reached over and stopped the video.

"A lot of work to deliver a pathetic poem. He had to get into the building and change, too."

"Yes, but security has been instructed to let people get to the apartment. Whoever he is realized the camera was aimed at my door. Abbie checked her phone. "I've gotta run. I'm meeting the mother-in-law-to-be for a luncheon with an aunt and a cousin and perhaps a couple others."

"So that's why you are dressed like that. I think the hat is a nice touch." Adam smirked.

"I don't need this from you. I am a nervous wreck as it is. I need to be likable but not too much, so no one is too hurt when I catch the stalker and end this farce."

Adam came around the desk and laid a hand on Abbie's shoulder. "You are sure you're not getting emotionally involved?"

Abbie met his concerned look. "Like I told Alex, I'm fine. Preston is a decent guy, and we have lines. His idea of following the protocol of Prince William and Kate is working. No more kissing. Only occasional touching as needed to escort me."

"Not what I asked."

"It isn't Preston. It's the fact I am so involved in his life. One of my bridesmaids is his fun and eccentric cousin. Now I am meeting his immediate family. I guess I pictured hanging out with just Preston all month."

"I don't talk much about September. I didn't see a relationship or whatever it was coming. There was no love at first sight. But the longer I watched over her, the closer we became. She nearly was killed because I was too blinded by my own feelings to see the danger. I know Alex is afraid you will fall for Preston—some curse-of-the-Art-House thing—but I am more concerned you'll get so sucked into the role you'll miss some clue and it'll be too late."

"I'm careful. I need to go." Abbie gave her brother a half hug and headed for her rental car. Next time she came to the office, she would need to be more careful. Someone could have followed her.

She had only seen what Preston referred to as "the residence" in photos. She had expected to talk into a call box to have the gate opened. Instead, two of Dermot's men emerged from a guard house to let her in and directed her to park next to a white Lamborghini. The Lexus she drove practically wilted in shame, poor little rental.

A butler met her at the door, and she felt the electronic extensions of the security guards watching her every step as she followed the older man through the foyer to a sitting room. Preston entered from another door.

"You decided to face the gauntlet." He took her hands and drew her closer, whispering in her ear. "Anything else from yesterday's note?"

Abbie shook her head and stepped back. "Nothing I haven't told you about." She smoothed her skirt and hoped she'd dressed acceptably.

Preston extended his arm. "I'll introduce you, then make myself scarce. Don't let them intimidate you." They had already discussed this. Gale's middle-class roots dismayed his mum. Gale's ignorance of her DAR worthiness compounded the problem in his great-aunt's eyes. As if qualifying for membership in the Daughters of the American Revolution mattered to a woman who still refused to give up her UK passport.

The five women stopped talking when Preston and Abbie stepped onto the veranda.

"Mum, I would like to introduce my fiancée, Miss Gale Henderson." He turned to Abbie, then went down the line. "My mother, Aunt Judith, you know Felicia, my great-aunt Josephine, and my second cousin Dorcas."

Abbie shook hands with each woman but was tempted to curtsy to Great-Aunt Josephine.

Preston kissed his mother's cheek and stage whispered, "Be nice to Gale. We have tickets to the theater tonight, and I don't want to go alone."

The women's laughter rang false to Abbie's ear. She followed them to a table where they were seated with the aid of the household staff. Abbie sat between Mrs. Harmon and Felicia.

"Preston tells me you don't drink alcohol. I hope you don't mind if we do. But I have asked our cook to make sure to have a selection of other drinks on hand. Just tell the server what you desire."

"Water with lime, please."

Felicia spoke. "Such simple tastes." Then she turned to the waiter. "Lemon seltzer."

When no one else ordered, Abbie figured their preferences were well-known.

Aunt Judith leaned forward. "So, how did you catch our boy's heart so quickly?"

"I believe they call it love at first sight for a reason, although it took me watching him fly a kite before my heart turned." Abbie was grateful when her water came. The salads followed.

Abbie blinked at hers. She had never seen anything like it.

Felicia leaned over and pointed with her fork. "They are all edible blooms. The honeysuckle is my favorite, although the nasturtium is delightful too."

Abbie picked up her fork, and Great-Aunt Josephine cleared her throat. "I believe it is appropriate to say grace before a meal."

The lengthy prayer offered by Great-Aunt Josephine left Felicia fidgeting next to her before the end. Abbie again picked up her salad fork.

"Try some of this dressing. It's our cook's secret recipe." Mrs. Harmon passed a crystal dressing bottle to Abbie.

As the first golden drops fell from the bottle, she saw one of the flowers move, then another. She set the dressing down and used her fork to move a spinach leaf to the side. A tiny face emerged, greeting her with a flickering tongue. "Well, hello, little guy. How did you get there?"

The simultaneous screams of Felicia and Mrs. Harmon and the scrape of chair legs against the tile were the only answers to Abbie's question.

"Snake!" shouted one of them.

Dorcas fanned Great-Aunt Josephine, who appeared to have fainted.

"Don't worry, he is only a little *opheodrys aestivus*, or green snake. Abbie lifted the six-inch-long snake from her plate. "If you will excuse me for a minute, I'll go find him a better home."

"Kill it!" screeched Mrs. Harmon.

"Whatever for? He isn't poisonous and is very beneficial in gardens." Abbie gently held the snake and stood.

Two security team members joined them.

"If one of you will point me in the direction of an appropriate garden, I'll help this little guy find a better lunch than my salad."

When she returned, the table had been cleared, and only Felicia remained.

"How could you touch it?"

"I had one as a pet when I was seven or eight. Is our luncheon over?" Abbie used her discarded napkin to wipe her hands.

"Yes, I am to send my regrets, but Aunt Margaret feels like it would be best to try another day."

It took Abbie a moment to realize Aunt Margaret was Mrs. Harmon. "Yes, too much excitement from a salad does ruin a meal."

One of the guards shadowed her all the way to the car. Preston failed to appear.

"How is your aunt?" Abbie weighed the rock she held in her palm.

Preston attempted to skip his across the pond. "Better today. Mum is still talking about you picking up the snake and walking into the garden. I am not sure what bothers her most—the snake or that you picked the slithery reptile up. To hear them tell the story, the *anaconda* you pulled out of the salad could have killed them all."

"I take it I didn't score any fiancée points."

"You did with Dad. He can't wait to meet you on his yacht tomorrow. Mum is going to be there too, and maybe Grandfather."

"So fewer witnesses if I don't pass muster?" Abbie's rock skipped nine times before sinking.

"I'd deny it, but Felicia is pretty much trying to talk me out of my rash decision to marry you at every turn. She likes you well enough but thinks you're too middle-class to fit in. I think she is torn about you. Usually she dislikes my girlfriends from the start." Felicia spent an hour telling him all the reasons why Gale was wrong for him while at the same time preparing for tonight's movie party with some of his friends. Preston would have been fine without the flavored popcorn and Italian soda bar, but Felicia wanted the party to be a success and insisted she be the one to throw it for the couple.

"I'm sorry my little green friend couldn't tell me how he ended up in the salad. I know this is frustrating to you and costing you a fortune preparing for a wedding that will never happen."

Preston's rock made it four skips. "How was your fitting this morning?"

"It went well. The dress is amazing, and it's only the model. What are you going to do with the real one?" Abbie studied Preston's profile. His forehead puckered.

"I hadn't thought about that. I retained Mateo when I expected the dress to be for Yvette. I suppose we can always use the gown in a spread to help launch his wedding collection."

"It isn't going to fit a model if he is making it for me, I am not exactly a size one."

Preston turned and faced her. "You could model it. With your bone structure and coloring, you would do well in print. Only runway models fit the old standard." He jestingly held his chin in his hand and walked slowly around her. "Not to be offensive or cross any lines, but your figure isn't bad either." It was good, but he best not let her know he was thinking just how attractive he found her. "I do prefer your natural eye color over the brown."

"Are you offering me a modeling job?" Abbie's cheeks pinked.

"Sure, why not?"

"I'm not the model type." Whether Abbie had bent down to search for another rock or to break out of the conversation, Preston couldn't be sure.

He squatted down beside her and reached over to move her hair out of her face. "I know you probably don't hear this working the job you do, but you are a beautiful woman."

She rolled her eyes. "You're only saying that because I'm your fiancée."

"Not true." He held her gaze as long as he could, hoping she believed him.

She nodded and stood. Her rock only skipped twice before sinking. "I guess we better head back. We do have a movie to watch."

He took her hand as they started on the path back to the main house. "Someday there will be a man who can make you believe it. Then I can tell you I told you so."

Her blush deepened. "Thanks, Preston. It does mean a lot coming from you."

At least she hadn't called him a liar.

eleven

CANDACE WRAPPED ANOTHER GAG GIFT for Araceli while Mandy watched. Zoe munched on a celery stick—her last-ditch effort at a diet before the wedding.

Mandy turned her attention to Abbie. "So, no closer to finding the stalker?"

"No, I hoped catching him would only take a week so I wouldn't have to be two people this weekend. The PIs discovered a girl-friend from four years ago. From her social media posts, she blames Preston for ruining her life. When she and Preston were dating, he walked in on her and a male photographer modeling their birthday suits to each other. Preston fired both of them. They went to Paris but couldn't get regular work. She started to eat all the chocolate croissants she could and tipped the scale at nearly three hundred pounds when she wrote the posts. However, the PI can't locate her or the photographer."

Mandy giggled. "That girl has a few problems, but I doubt Preston was one of them. How serious were they?"

"According to Preston, they had only gone out once and it was a disaster."

Candace packed the last gift into a suitcase. "Any other prom-ising candidates?"

"The PIs have eliminated most. There are the usual vague, anonymous threats and such. Which brings me back to my dual identity. Araceli's wedding is going to be entertaining. Zoe, you are in charge of making sure I put in my contacts and extensions every time I leave you guys."

"I looked at a map. At least the two hotels are close. It should only take you a few minutes to get from one to the other. Just don't change in the back of the taxi," said Mandy.

"I told Preston I intend to have a case of food poisoning after Thursday's lunch so no one will get suspicious when I don't come out of my room until Saturday morning."

Candace looked up from her package. "You know, I like Preston a lot more than I did two weeks ago. I didn't think he was really human. He seemed so detached. But making it possible for you to go to the wedding is decent of him."

"He is trying to make the best of this. I thought he was just buying himself a solution, but after his apology for the engagement kiss—"

Mandy sat up. "Wait! What?"

Candace scowled. "Lie back down before your mom or Daniel come in here and make us leave. Abbie explain."

This had been why she hadn't told them last week when the proposal happened. "Last Monday night after the proposal, we went back to my apartment. He was agitated. It turns out he felt bad about paying me to kiss him. Since then he has only kissed me on the cheek a couple times, mostly around his family, like on the yacht Saturday."

"That is so sweet!" Zoe bounced off her chair.

Abbie looked at her hands, waiting for the inevitable blush to settle. Best to change the subject. "So, you guys will get me checked into the Four Seasons and have my suitcase, and I'll come over Wednesday for a bit. Then I am all yours Thursday, from three until the happy couple leaves." Her phone pinged. "I'd better go. Adam and Alex are meeting me at the apartment.

They are a bit upset about this job, so I am letting them have a sit-down with Preston."

She hugged Mandy and the others. Candace followed her to the elevator. "How invested is your heart in this?"

"Not much. It's hard to play dress up for the fake wedding. Margaret, Preston's mom, took me to pick out china patterns yesterday afternoon. Get to know the mother-in-law time, and since there were no snakes in sight, things went well. She is formal with me, but she is a Brit. Which might explain the ugly pattern she wants me to get."

"Not what I asked."

The elevator bell dinged.

"I know, but don't worry about me. He isn't leading me on or anything. Sometimes I wish he was the person I thought he was when we met. This job would be easier if he were arrogant." *And if I didn't spend so much time wondering why Yvette said he was a bad kisser. The one we had was better than good, even if his heart wasn't in it...*

Preston entered the elevator in Abbie's building with the pizza-delivery guy, hoping the pizza was the order for their meeting. He had been party to a hostile takeover or two in his career, and food usually helped keep tempers down. The meeting with Abbie's brothers demanded a meal. When they reached Abbie's floor, the pizza guy pushed his way past Preston and rushed to Abbie's door, so Preston hung back and waited until the transaction was finished before stepping in through the open door.

Abbie smiled at him. "Come on back. My brothers are in the kitchen impatiently waiting with the other pizza. I guess we double ordered."

He braced himself for the inevitable masculine showdown with the two men in her kitchen. They did the same Hastings intimidating stare their father, and, on occasion, Abbie used, as if dissecting him, searching for some weakness or ulterior motive.

"Adam, Alex, back down. He is a client, so stop the games." Abbie set the box down with the others, then stepped over and hugged her twin. Alex's stare softened a fraction. "You have already met Alex. This is my oldest brother, Adam."

Adam extended his hand, the handshake firm but not painful. "Nice to meet you."

"Sorry, Preston, I guess I should have written FAKE in all caps for their memo. My brothers may have taken one too many to the head. Let's sit down and eat. No one needs to defend my honor here." Abbie pulled four plates out of the cupboard and set them on the table. Alex grabbed bottles of water out of the fridge.

They sat and passed around the pizzas.

"Who ordered the veggie with mushrooms? Alex?" Abbie looked at her brothers and took a slice. Both brothers shook their heads. Abbie opened her mouth to take a bite.

"Stop!" Preston grabbed her wrist and yanked the pizza away from her mouth.

Alex stood so fast his chair shot several feet across the floor.

"What?" Abbie looked at him, the pizza still in her hand.

"The mushrooms are the wrong shape." Preston released her wrist. "Your brothers didn't order that pizza, and I didn't. You must not have, or you wouldn't have asked."

Abby dropped the slice onto her plate, blanching at the realization that someone had bypassed their security, no warning this time.

Adam put the pizza slices back in the box. "This was the one that showed up late, wasn't it?"

Abby nodded.

Adam took charge. "Alex, get a garbage bag. We can get the mushrooms analyzed. Abbs, was it the same guy who delivered the first pizza?"

"No, he was taller. Looked like he might work out. I don't think he wore the red shirt under his jacket. The cap was low over his sunglasses so I didn't see his face." Abby took a drink of her water.

"Preston, you were on the elevator with him. Did you notice anything?" asked Adam.

"He wore sunglasses with the baseball cap. Most people take them off inside, but the pizza smelled so good I didn't think anything of it."

Abbie stood and left the room. Preston got up to follow her, but Alex cut him off. "She's my twin. I'll go."

Adam sat back down. "How did you realize the mushrooms were the wrong shape?"

"One summer, years ago, my cousin wanted to be a mycologist. She collected all sorts of plants and fungi and kept them in our greenhouse as my aunt didn't like her hobby. She was forever talking about them. I guess I remembered something. I can't even tell you what kind they are." Preston looked at the pizza on his plate, but his appetite was gone.

"Any chance your cousin could be the stalker?" asked Adam.

Preston tried to picture his cousin running off his girlfriends. "Not a chance." She liked most of them but didn't think they were right for him. Felicia liked Abbie better than all of them. What would be the point? "My getting married doesn't affect her inheritance. Besides, she has always been my best bud."

Abbie's phone pinged. Preston looked at the screen, the message still visible: **Hope you enjoyed the pizza. Don't worry, the cramping and nausea will only last a day. Break up with Preston, and I'll text you the cure.**

Preston read the text to Adam. Adam grabbed the phone and left the room. They all joined him in the living room.

Abbie sat on the couch next to Preston. "Thanks for stopping me."

"Are you all right? I didn't hurt your wrist?"

Abbie laughed. "No, I grew up with them." She nodded to her brothers. "I'm upset I let my guard down. I just—"

77

Alex crossed his arms. "You shouldn't have taken this job."

"Don't you dare tell—"

Adam stepped between the twins. "Alex, you are not always very objective when it comes to Abbie. Why don't you deliver the pizza to the office so it can get out to a lab tonight?"

Alex grunted but complied.

Adam waited until he left before continuing. "The stalker has just escalated the game. None of us were expecting it. I know you two are leaving for Boston tomorrow. I don't want trouble following you there. Preston, what kind of security are you taking?"

"Just a two-person tag team. I am going to be in meetings most of Wednesday, Thursday, and Friday to cover for Abbie not being with me. On Saturday we'll go out to Martha's Vineyard to the cottage and come back Sunday night."

"Do you know who the team will be?"

"No, but after I tell Simon about this, I doubt he will assign the type of person Abbie wanted."

Adam turned to his sister. "What did you request?"

"Someone who might not notice me slipping in and out of the hotel," said Abbie.

"Abbie, do you know if Kyle Evans will have a security team there for his wedding?"

"He should. With a high-profile wedding, he would want to keep the paparazzi at bay, if nothing else. Araceli's family isn't exactly used to the spotlight. They aren't even announcing the location until the morning of the wedding and then only to RSVPed guests."

Adam drummed his fingers on the arm of his chair. "I suppose you have contact information for his team since you and Alex were originally going to go with the Crawfords. I'd like to talk to the head of the Evans detail to give them a heads-up."

"You want eyes on me in Boston?" Abbie raised her brows.

"That, and if the stalker knows your food preferences, what else would they know?"

Abbie pulled out her phone and handed it to her brother. "Meet my fake profile. It states my favorite food is veggie-mushroom pizza, which makes me doubly stupid for forgetting I put my food preferences on there."

"Nice work. I assume Alan set up the page and you have years of posts." Adam looked at Preston. "So that you know, I am only slightly less protective of my sister than Alex is. The kissing-in-the-restaurant photo of your engagement on social media isn't my favorite. But unlike Alex, I understand the necessity. I also know from experience how an undercover job can mess with all the players as the lines of reality blur. You both need to keep things professional."

Preston ignored the lump that inevitably came whenever one of the Hastings glared at him. "I know. I'm sorry. I have already apologized."

"So she says, but she conveniently shut off the audio." Adam stood up and went to the TV. "Hey, do you think we got pizza guy or his voice on tape?"

Abbie walked over and put her hand on her brother's shoulder. "Adam, not now. Look when you get to the office in the morning. I don't want to spend the entire evening analyzing what I missed when it has already been a long day."

Adam pulled her into a hug. "Okay. I'll take that as my hint to go. Bye, sis." He kissed her on the forehead and left.

Abbie turned to Preston. "Are you hungry?"

"Not really. Do you want to go someplace?"

Abbie shook her head. "No, but I don't want to be alone yet, either."

"If I go home now, the stalker could get the wrong message. We could watch a movie. Don't worry. I know your brothers are watching. I'll be professional."

She picked up the remote. "I am not worried, even if they weren't watching. We are friends." She sat next to him on the couch. "Romantic comedy?"

"Sounds good."

By the time the couple in the movie got together, Abbie was softly curled into his side and snoring. Usually, he watched movies in his home theater, with its leather recliners, or at a premier. Having a woman use him as a pillow during a film was not a common experience. The closing credits rolled.

Abbie woke up. She opened her eyes and sat up, pushing back her hair. "I'm sorry, I shouldn't have—"

He put his finger to her lips. "Don't apologize. Thank you for letting me watch. Next time we can watch something you can stay awake for."

She walked him to the door.

"I'll send a car around three o'clock to take us to the airport." He leaned down and touched his lips to her cheek. The brothers would probably be annoyed, but he didn't care.

twelve

ABBIE CHECKED TO MAKE SURE neither of Preston's bodyguards had followed her. After conferring with Simon Dermot the other evening, Simon had decided to come himself. Unfortunately, Patrick had ended up as the second guard after Simon's original choice came down with a stomach bug an hour before they were scheduled to leave. So far Simon had kept Patrick looking the other way when Gale needed to become Abbie. She crossed the bottom of the Boston Common and onto Boylston Street.

Candace, Tessa, and Zoe were sorting items in the sitting room of their suite. "You made it."

"Give me a minute to get rid of my extensions and brown eyes. I am ready to be me for the next day and a half."

"Araceli called. She will be here in an hour. Don't forget to put on your colored extensions." Candace twirled a lock of her own multicolored wig.

The bride arrived and the party started. Abbie took photos of the toilet-paper wedding dresses. Candace won again.

Mandy laughed over the video conference. "How do you do it? That one's even better than the one you created for my party."

Candace made Araceli twirl. "I have an eye."

"So your next major will be fashion design?" asked Tessa.

"Not likely. The department gave me a choice—come teach full time or move on."

"Dr. Christensen told you that?" asked Mandy.

"No, the dean. I have until July 15 to decide what I want to do. If I teach, I get almost all 100-level classes, and I have to have natural-colored hair." Candace posed Araceli for another photo. "Now, let's see if I can get you out of this so you can put it on again," she joked.

"Again?"

"I am sure you and Kyle can find something to do with it," said Mandy, playing along.

Zoe leaned into the phone's camera. "What did you do with yours?"

Mandy laughed. "I could tell you, but then I would have to send Alex after you."

Araceli turned beet red.

Someone knocked on the door.

Zoe opened it. "Mrs. Williams, come in. We were finishing up."

"I stopped by to let Araceli know we are back and to remind her you all need your beauty sleep."

"Thanks, Mom. I'll be up to our suite in just a few."

Mrs. Williams left.

One last round of hugs, and Mandy signed off on her end.

Araceli gathered up her gifts and left.

Candace gathered up her things. "Well, Tessa, you are next."

Tessa helped clean up. "Sean's grandfather was in the hospital last week. Sean wants the option of moving our wedding up if he thinks his grandfather is failing again. Of course, Reverend Cavanagh claims he'll live until the Christmas program. He has five great grandchildren. It is such a special time for him, and Sean thinks we should wait for the season. I am holding out for the date we picked so my father can be there since his wife will have their baby by then. But I am worried about Sean's grandfather, I know he thinks he can recover quickly but he is over eighty."

"Then he will," said Candace. "You would be surprised how much prayer and positive thinking can do." For a moment, Abbie thought Candace's voice caught and there might have been a tear in her eye, but the moisture disappeared as fast as it came.

Zoe gathered the plastic cups. "Do you have a dress yet?"

"No. I thought you guys would like to come down to NYC on Saturday and look."

"I can't, but if you want to come out to Chicago, I know a great designer," said Abbie.

Tessa sat opposite Abbie. "Explain. What is going on?"

Abbie told a condensed version of her job for Preston.

"What happens if the wedding date gets here and you haven't caught the stalker?"

"Then we go ahead with a fake marriage. Preston is hiring an actor to play the minister and some other things. He booked a two-room suite in Hawaii, so I have a separate room."

"Whoa, how far will you take this?" Zoe perched on the arm of the chair Tessa sat in.

"Considering the pizza incident on Monday, we don't think the search will take that long. Things are escalating. But Preston can't make it look like any part of our relationship is a hoax. He and the head of security are covering for me through tomorrow night. It is unlikely the stalker followed us here anyway. But Adam did let the Evans's security team know in case."

Candace sat down and pulled off her wig. "Well, ladies, it's time for us to get some sleep."

In her bathroom, Abbie took off her colorful extensions and laid them next to the ones she used as Gale. Real or fake, fake or real? One should not try to be philosophical after midnight.

She turned off the light.

Preston took off his tie. The meetings had gone well, but the dinner had been insufferable. No matter how many times he reminded Miss Banks he was engaged, she kept trying to get his attention. The half dozen times he removed her hand from his knee during the salad course made it difficult to eat. Only Patrick's presence had prevented her from following Preston up to his hotel room. He'd missed Abbie's conversation.

He picked up his phone and texted her.

How are you feeling?

— **Tired. I knew the lobster was a bad choice. Were your meetings successful?**

Preston wondered how she really was. The hen party should be over soon. He pictured her laughing with the two friends he'd met last week at the film party.

Mostly. Some things must be ironed out tomorrow. Do you think you might be up to going out tomorrow night to the Boston Opera House?

— **Opera?**

No there is a Broadway musical playing.

— **Can you get tickets on such short notice?**

— **I reserved them 2 weeks ago.** It seemed like a logical choice as they needed to be seen together in public.

You never said you were a Boy Scout. You have that be-prepared thing down.

Preston laughed. **Ha, Ha. No. I'm just my grandfather's protégé.**

— **What time?**

8

— **I think I should be recovered by then. Just don't make me eat any seafood.**

Deal. Let me know if you feel well enough for dinner too.

— **I will.**

Good night. Dream of me.

— **Is that the equivalent of sweet dreams? :)**

Yup. *Maybe.*

He had found Abbie in his dreams more often. In some of them, the stalker won. Those were not sweet.

— Good night to you too.

Preston stared at his screen. If they were really getting married, he would have written something else. But writing the three little words on the off chance someone would read their conversation seemed wrong. He had never told Yvette he loved her. It would have been a lie, their relationship having resembled a business merger. She didn't love him as much as she did his money. Abbie was a friend. Perhaps the first true friend he'd had in a while.

The irony wasn't lost on him, though. The best friendship he'd had in years was fake.

thirteen

FEELING MUCH BETTER. I CAN go out by six.

Abbie left the afternoon reception with the bridal party shortly after Araceli and Kyle. Candace, Tessa, and Zoe sat in the limo with her in their matching seafoam dresses. She didn't feel left out in her blue skirt and jacket.

Zoe sighed. "She looked so happy. I hope I can find someone who makes me smile like a sunny day."

"My mother had a friend who didn't wear any makeup on her wedding day because her husband made her feel so beautiful she didn't think she needed it. I wonder how that kind of love feels," said Candace.

Abbie's thoughts flew to her conversation with Preston by the pond. The way he had looked at her, she'd almost believed him. Not enough to toss her mascara in the trash, but maybe enough to model one useless wedding dress.

Tessa's laugh interrupted Abbie's musings. "Sean makes me feel beautiful, but there is no way I am standing up in front of a hundred people without my lipstick and eyeliner."

Candace shifted in her rear-facing seat. "The funny thing is, Mom said her friend wasn't a cover girl or anything, just average.

I'd settle for a guy who could look at me without the wigs and makeup and not wince."

"Colin has seen you without your wig," said Zoe.

"Several men have seen me wearing scarves, including Colin, but that isn't the same as bald." Candace turned to Abbie in an obvious attempt to change the subject. "What are you and Preston doing tonight?"

"He got tickets to the musical playing at the Boston Opera House."

Tessa looked up the show on her phone. "Sean took me to that on my visit to New York during spring break. I still wake up humming the love song."

"Not sure that means much. You woke up every morning humming some love song." Abbie looked out the window as the limo slowed. "We're here now. Time to turn into Gale again."

At the Four Seasons, Abbie hurried to change back into her Gale hair and clothes. Her phone beeped.

— I'll be back at the hotel in twenty minutes.

I should be in my room. Taking a walk now.

Abbie packed her clothes and makeup for Candace to take back to Chicago. The others were still in their rooms, so she called out her goodbyes before heading back across the common.

The Ritz doorman opened the door for her as the car service pulled up to the curb.

Preston hopped out, followed by Patrick. Preston hurried to her side and looped his arm around her waist. "I am glad to see you up and walking." He propelled her across the lobby and whispered, "Your eyes are a lovely shade of blue."

Patrick caught up with them at the bank of elevators.

Abbie's mind raced. Where had she left her brown contacts? In her purse. At least she had them with her. But she couldn't risk Patrick seeing.

On the elevator, she turned her back to Patrick and played with Preston's tie. "How did your meetings go today?"

"As smoothly as can be expected. Shall we catch a quick dinner before the theater or order room service?"

Abbie ran her fingers along one of the silk stripes of the tie, aware Patrick was listening to every word. "I think room service would be best. I need to change and fix my face."

"I like it the way it is, but if you say so." The elevator reached their floor. Patrick checked Preston's room, then went down the hall to the room he shared with Simon.

Abbie opened her door. Preston leaned against the jamb. "Do you mind if I order dinner up to my room?"

"No." Abbie noticed a large trademark turquoise-blue box on the table. "Preston, you shouldn't have." She lifted the lid.

"I didn't." He took a step into the room.

"Stop!" Dread filled Abbie when she saw the contents of the box. "Send Simon in here, and you and Patrick leave the floor. Pull the fire alarm once you reach the lobby. When you are outside, call 911."

"Gale?"

"It's a bomb. Go now!"

"I can't leave—"

"This is my job! Get out of here!" Abbie whirled on him and pushed him out the door. She didn't turn back into her suite until Preston was pounding on the door to the room down the hall the security team used. Then she reached inside her purse and pulled out her pocket knife and cell phone, debating only a second before linking a video call to her brother.

"Adam, I have an emergency."

Standing outside the hotel waiting for Boston's finest was not where Preston wanted to be, but Patrick had a firm hand on his shoulder so he wouldn't go running back into the building.

Patrick interrupted his thoughts. "Why hasn't Simon brought your fiancée down?"

The lie came quickly to Preston's mind, probably from some movie script. "I don't know. Gale thought she stepped on something that clicked when she opened the box. She refused to move in case it was a pressure plate. I think she watches too much TV." There was no way the bodyguard would believe such an inane tale, but Patrick nodded and studied the building.

Preston looked at his watch. How much time was left on the timer? The phone attached to the bomb didn't have large numbers like on TV. Police and fire trucks pulled up. The hotel manager pointed one of the policemen to him.

The policeman jogged over. "Sergeant Rourke. Are you the one who reported this?"

"Yes, there was a box on her table, and my fiancée opened it, and we think it's a bomb."

"Where is she?"

How could he explain without Patrick figuring out Abbie's dual identity? Another policeman came up and addressed Patrick. The bodyguard let go of Preston's shoulder. Preston walked around the sergeant and pointed to the third floor from the top. "She is up there with my head of security."

The officer swore.

Preston checked to make sure Patrick couldn't hear, then looked the sergeant in the eye. "She's former Secret Service. He's a retired Seal."

The sergeant nodded and ran off. While other officers and firefighters urged the hotel evacuees toward the Boston Common, Preston stayed close to Patrick and prayed.

Simon Dermot studied the bomb and the abnormalities Adam and Abbie pointed out. "I believe you're right. It looks like a fake. The C-4 is some sort of modeling clay, and the wires are too haphazard."

"Four minutes, Adam. What should we do?" she shouted over the fire alarm.

"I wish I could smell over the phone. Then I would know for sure. Tug lightly on the yellow wire. It looks like it isn't even connected to the blasting cap."

Simon did the honors, and the wire slid out of the cap.

"Okay, now pull out the cap. Look for a logo." Adam's worried face filled Abbie's screen.

Abbie held the cap up to the phone. "There it is, near the crimp."

"Do you recognize it, Abbie? I think it's the same company I buy our training kits from."

Simon took the cap from Abbie. "I have used this brand too."

Abbie took a deep breath.

The pounding of feet down the hallway was nearly as loud as the alarm.

"Gotta go." She turned the phone off.

"Step away from the bomb."

Simon faced the officers and held his hands up in a calming motion. "It's defused."

"What is the situation?" demanded a uniformed officer. Mercifully, the sound of the fire alarm stopped.

Simon pulled the last of the wires. "It's a movie-set prop."

When the timer on the phone attached to the dummy bomb reached zero, the phone rang a shrill tone, making everyone in the room jump. The speaker activated without anyone touching it.

"Kaboom!" yelled a mechanical voice, followed by inhuman laughter. "This time you didn't lose your pretty face, nor did he lose his. But this movie prop cost me almost as much as the real thing. Give back the ring or face the consequences." Computerized laughter filled the room.

The officer joined Abbie and Simon where they stood near the table. "I'm Sergeant Rourke. Can you explain what this is?"

Abbie spoke first. "My stalker is escalating again."

"You'd better explain, miss, while the bomb squad takes a look at this thing."

"Sure, but don't destroy it. Maybe we can finally get a clue." Abbie told the officer what she knew.

The bomb squad removed the inert bomb, Abbie and Simon gave their statements, and everyone left the room. Then Abbie rushed into the bathroom to put in her brown contacts and hoped Simon could come up with something to tell Patrick.

Patrick used his keycard to open Abbie's door. Preston crossed the room in three strides and pulled Abbie into a hug while Patrick hovered in the doorway.

"A little privacy, please."

"Yes, Mr. Harmon."

Preston didn't talk until he heard the click of the door. "Of all the stupid things. You should have left with me."

Abbie stepped out of his embrace. "I was doing my job."

"But you could have—"

She shook her head. "When you hired me to do this, we both knew there could be danger. Today we were lucky and were in no more danger than any A-list Hollywood actor."

"When you pushed me out of the room, I wanted to drag you out too, but I knew you could—" He waved his hands helplessly. This time the lump in his throat came for an entirely different reason. "I don't have many real friends in this world. This isn't worth having you die."

Abbie placed her hand over his heart. "I have no intention of dying. If Simon, Adam, and I hadn't figured the bomb out in the first three minutes, I would have evacuated."

Preston tucked a lock of hair behind her ear and looked into her eyes. Brown. He preferred her real eye color and the real her. This wasn't just friends anymore. He stepped closer and ran his fingers down the side of her face. Abbie leaned into his touch. "Abbie, I—"

When the first notes of the William Tell Overture interrupted him, she stepped out of his arms and answered the phone. "Hi, Dad. Don't worry. We're fine."

No, we are not. Preston left her alone to talk with her father.

fourteen

THE LIGHTS OF BOSTON GREW smaller through the jet window.
Simon Dermot and Jethro Hastings determined the rest of the
weekend plans should be scrapped. The management of the
Ritz wasn't exactly sad to see them check out early. Preston had
promised to take Abbie to the missed show after they caught the
stalker regardless of where they had to fly. She traced a line of
lights on the window and wondered what might have happened
if her father hadn't called. But she knew. Adrenaline and high
emotions would have taken over, and she would have confused
the momentary safety she'd found in his arms for something
lasting. Adam had warned her. So had Alex.

Letting her relationship with Mandy get personal was a mistake,
but she cherished that friendship. She wouldn't mind not being
Mandy's bodyguard since the trade-off was worth it.

If she had allowed Preston the kiss, she would have kissed
him back—and she would be useless to him. As she replayed
the events of the evening in her mind, things she hadn't noticed
before surfaced. She turned her attention to the other passengers.
Simon Dermot and Patrick sat at the front of the plane watching
a game on the television. Preston sat across from her, looking
out his window. Abbie unbuckled her seat belt and stood. She

tapped Preston on the shoulder and beckoned him to the rear of the plane.

The master suite would suit her purposes. With a TV, bathroom, and walk-in shower, she had multiple options to keep what she needed to say private. Preston raised his brows when she shut the door. Abbie put her finger to her lips to keep him from talking while she looked for the remote. Unable to find it, she turned to Preston. "Want to show me your onboard movie collection?"

Preston opened a drawer and pulled out the remote. "Comedy or romance?"

"Romantic comedy?" Abbie pointed at a movie she had seen a half dozen times with her friends. Once the movie started, she beckoned Preston into the bathroom, hoping the noise of the TV would drown out any conversation. "Any chance your security team records or can hear what is going on in here?"

"I don't think so. Why?"

"Because I think I know how the bomb got in the room."

The plane dipped, and Preston grabbed Abbie's arm. "Let's go sit on the bed. I'd rather not hit my head on the sink in here."

Abbie followed him out to the bed and sat close to him so she could whisper. "After the all-clear, how did you get into my room?"

"Patrick used his key card."

"Simon told me Patrick wouldn't have a card to my room. How did he get it? Did he take it when you left the floor?"

Preston closed his eyes. "No, he started to argue with Simon about who should go, but he stopped when Simon ran out of the room. I didn't see Patrick pick up anything, so he must have had the keycard with him."

Abbie closed her eyes and pictured other events. "When we came up to the rooms before I found the bomb, Patrick cleared your room, but he didn't wait for me to open my door to check my room. Which has been Simon's protocol the entire trip. How long was Patrick with you today?"

"He wasn't in the negotiation room. Since the office was secure, there was no problem. I didn't see him until our lunch break."

"Where was Simon during the day?"

"He stayed at the hotel, supposedly to guard you."

Simon was keeping Patrick from realizing she wasn't in the room.

Abby ran her hands over her face. "Both men had access and no alibi for at least part of the day. But Patrick shouldn't have had access at all, and Simon knows who I am. I am going to assume who ever put the box on the table never opened the door to the bedroom, or he would have known I wasn't in there recovering from the lobster." She closed her eyes picturing the room as she found it. The bed was still unmade, so housekeeping hadn't come in, and she'd had to unlock the bathroom door —locking the door was an extra layer of the "sickness" cover she'd added in case someone came in, hoping they would assume she was in the tub.

Preston stared at her. "Are you saying … ?"

"I think so. The pizza guy the other night. How close in build would you say he is to Patrick?"

"No way." Preston stood, but Abbie pulled him back onto the bed.

"The guard who was supposed to come with Simon to Boston took ill, and Patrick replaced him at the last minute. Do you know any details about that?"

"Other than Wednesday was supposed to be Patrick's day off, not really."

"Where did Patrick get reassigned?"

"My uncle's, I think."

They sat in silence as the movie couple managed to get themselves in another predicament.

Preston stood to leave.

Abbie touched his arm. "You can't leave until the movie is over, or it will look odd."

He sat back down. "You know what your protectors will do to me if they realize I spent ninety minutes of the flight locked in a bedroom with you."

Abbie laughed. "I won't let them. Now, we need a plan. Patrick must realize by now that something is off with me. I shouldn't have stayed with the bomb, but at the time it seemed like the right thing."

"I think he believed the story I told him, though it was a bit too Hollywood. But the fact that you pick up snakes may make him wonder." Preston made a mock horrified face before turning serious. "I can't believe he is the stalker. Are you sure?"

"More likely he works for the stalker. He doesn't have a motive to break up your relationships, and believe me, he doesn't have a romantic interest in you."

"How do you know?"

"He definitely prefers females."

"Did he ever prefer you?"

"Let's just leave it at the fact that Patrick knows firsthand how protective my brothers can be." For some reason, they had taken a peculiar interest in keeping Patrick out of her life. Except for Alex, they mostly let her choose her boyfriends and stayed out if it. It was hard enough getting a third date once her career became a topic of conversation.

Preston frowned. "I should fire him just for whatever he did to you."

Abbie patted his shoulder. "It's only been words for years. Nothing I can't handle myself, but thank you for caring."

Preston leaned back against the headboard. "What now?"

"We wait. You walk me up to my apartment, where my dad and at least one brother are probably already pacing." Abbie sat next to Preston until the movie ended, and they retook their seats for landing, Abbie doing her best to pretend both bodyguards weren't there.

No one was pacing when Abbie opened her apartment door. Instead, all stood with their arms folded as Preston brought her bag in. Before anyone could speak, Abbie held up her hand. "One: he who gives Preston any flack will be kicked out of this meeting and will be challenged to a round in the gym. Be warned, I am angry, and I haven't had a good spar in over two weeks. Two: you are all going to give me ten minutes alone. Three: you will wait for me before this officially begins." She grabbed her bag and walked into the bedroom.

Jethro took a seat and indicated for Preston to do the same. Adam and Alex took their places on one couch. The two brothers Preston hadn't met sat on the other.

Adam spoke. "Has she been this angry the entire flight?"

"If she was, she hid her emotions well." Preston turned to the other brothers. "I assume you are Alan and Andrew."

The brothers nodded, leaving him to guess who was who. Knowing Andrew was younger than Abbie, he hoped he chose correctly.

Jethro spoke. "My daughter can hide her emotions well when she needs to. With four brothers teasing her, she learned fast. I'm surprised she didn't vent on the flight home."

"She had her reasons not to, and I think it's best we wait before I say more. You all may be able to stand up to her in the gym, but I don't think I dare find out if I can."

Alex laughed. "Wise man. She plays dirty and has taken us all down at one time or another."

Preston leaned forward placing elbows on his knees. "One question: What is her history with Patrick Vonn?"

All the brothers leaned forward simultaneously. Preston thought he heard them growl too. "What did the slime do this time?" Adam's eyes narrowed.

Preston's gut knotted. This was how the receiving end of their wrath felt.

"Boys." At the single word from Jethro, they all relaxed. "In high school, Patrick made a locker-room bet about how far he could force her to go and bragged he would drag her to home base. Andrew overheard, and the boys took things into their own hands, and Patrick has relied on innuendo and rumor for most of his retaliation against Abbie since he wasn't able to win that bet."

"How come none of you told me?" Abbie stood in the doorway in jeans and a T-shirt, drying her hair with a towel. "All these years I thought Alex overreacted because Patrick tried to kiss me. Had I known about the bet, I never would have gone on that date and would have decked him myself."

Alex shrugged. "At the time his motives weren't something any of us felt comfortable telling you about. We only told Dad after the fact to save ourselves from being grounded for a year."

Abbie huffed and walked back into the bedroom.

"And a decade later, Patrick is still trying to win the bet," Adam muttered.

Preston would not only fire Patrick, he would make sure he left Chicago.

Abbie returned with her hair in a ponytail. "I guess I should have left you with a fourth stipulation not to discuss me, but under the circumstances, I assume Preston started it with a more than fair question about Patrick." She took a seat in the space between Adam and Alex. Preston regretted not sitting on a couch.

"What do you mean? Preston didn't tell us what Patrick did."

"Abbie thinks Patrick is in league with the stalker, and her reasoning is sound." Preston repeated most of their conversation from the airplane.

Alex turned to his twin. "Do you think he knows who you are?"

Abbie shrugged. "He leered at me after Preston and I came out of the airplane bedroom." She immediately put a restraining hand on her brother's arm. "My idea, not Preston's. I figured between the closed door and the sounds of the TV, we could talk privately."

Alex sat back but still gave Preston a warning look.

Jethro rubbed his chin. "There is also the outside possibility the culprit was Simon."

"I thought of that, but he seemed as perplexed by the bomb as I was, and he knows my identity. Adam, you saw him on the video. What do you think?" asked Abbie.

"I agree the bomb surprised him."

"Simon wouldn't risk his reputation for something so trivial as mostly harmless pranks against girlfriends. My guess is he is wondering the same thing we are." Jethro stood and walked to the window. "If we bring Patrick in, he isn't likely to talk, and that still leaves the stalker to pay someone else off. If we don't isolate him somehow and he tells the stalker Gale is Abbie, things could escalate dangerously."

"I think we need to figure out if Patrick knows I'm me or I'm Gale." Abbie waved her hand. "You know what I mean."

"How do we do that?" asked Adam.

"There hasn't been a time in the last thirteen years he hasn't let some lewd comment out of his mouth when we've crossed paths at some event or another. If he runs into me as me, he won't be able to refrain from saying something. There is some charity brunch tomorrow." Abbie looked at her phone. "I mean today. Mandy received an invitation to the benefit as it has to do with a children's charity. She hoped the doctor would give her clearance to go. Alex, do you know if she can?"

"As long as she is in a wheelchair. Daniel is going too."

"Great. You were already working the brunch. No problem getting me in." Abbie smiled and turned her head. "Preston, I assume someone in your family would be scheduled to attend. Either your mother or an aunt. So we need Simon to assign Patrick to that duty."

Alex folded his arms. "I don't like it. If Patrick does know, he may do more than say something."

Adam moved forward in his seat. "I'll go too. We have done three-person teams before, and Patrick won't know that we don't have another client."

"It is better to have an extra guard there anyway if something happens and the Crawfords need us. I don't want everyone distracted." Jethro leaned against the window. "I'm going to send Mark Gowen in rather than Alex. Mark has worked with the Crawfords before and can make them his number-one priority."

"But—" Alex and Adam tried to interrupt.

Jethro didn't allow his sons to argue. "Alex, I can't afford to have you there with Abbie. You tend to punch first and ask questions later where she is concerned. Besides, you haven't had a full day off in weeks since you have been on call for hospital runs with Mandy. Let Abbie cover for you."

"Now is not the time to say this, but I need to be pulled from Mandy's detail probably permanently." Abbie gave a weak smile.

"I know, but not until after the baby comes. Mandy doesn't need to get used to a new person right now. And there is more to her safety than restraining a half-crazed woman who thinks she should be Daniel's baby's mama."

Preston was impressed by the Hastings' foresight and wondered if Simon thought of such things when he made his plans.

"One thing more," said Abbie. "Patrick knows Gale is back in the city. He needs to think I am someplace else."

"I can come here to pick you up for an outing a half hour before the event," Preston offered. "Then, if he looks at the master schedule, it will show I'm with you."

"You'll need to stay here, or your driver will know I'm not around. I am sure there is something wedding related we need to do for three hours. Revise the guest list? Change your mother's china choice? It's ghastly."

Everyone laughed.

Jethro looked at his watch. "It's nearly one. I'll call Simon at oh six hundred and let you know if any changes need to be made."

Abbie hugged everyone, including Preston, as they left. Jethro and his sons shook Preston's hand. Only Alex's grip came close to breaking any bones. Preston considered that a good thing.

fifteen

ABBIE STIFLED A YAWN. FALLING asleep on the job was unacceptable. The temporary blonde spray dye had lightened her hair enough to impress Adam when she met him at the Crawford's Saturday morning in a pantsuit that allowed her the freedom of movement the dresses of the last couple of weeks had limited. Looking around the banquet hall at the women dressed in spring and summer fabrics, Abbie almost wished she could have worn something more feminine.

Acquaintances were gathered around Mandy's chair, expressing congratulations and passing on motherly wisdom. All of them were familiar faces. On the far side of the room, Great-Aunt Josephine and Felicia sat at one of the front tables. They looked in Abbie's direction. She hoped they didn't see the resemblance. Felicia waved very properly to one of her friends. Abbie assumed Felicia didn't see her any more than she did the wait staff refilling coffee cups.

When the chairwoman stood and called the meeting to order, the few bodyguards in the room took up their posts along the perimeter, close to their various clients. Patrick was leaning against the far wall. This was not going to be easy.

Daniel, one of the few men in attendance, signaled her as the wait staff started serving the fruit plates. Abbie went to the couple.

"Baby kicked the wrong place," whispered Mandy.

Abbie wheeled Mandy to the closest accessible restroom. After seeing Mandy safely inside, she took up her position outside the room.

"If it isn't the virtuous Miss Hastings. I haven't seen you around for three or four weeks."

"Go away, Patrick. I'm working."

"You know, my employer is engaged to a woman who reminds me of you. A true doppelgänger. Only, looking at you I see I was mistaken. She fills out a dress in a way you never could." Patrick slowly assessed her from toe to hair.

"I'm sure your employer appreciates you lusting after his fiancée. Maybe I should tell him?"

"He might not mind. He goes through women fast enough, and seeing she joined his mile-high club last night, who knows how fast he'll dump her." Patrick's grin was enough to make Abbie gag. He stepped closer. "I know she can't be you. 'Cause you are too uptight to let anyone in those pants of yours." When Patrick reached out to pat her posterior, Abbie got the satisfaction of trying one of the moves she'd perfected on her brothers.

Thump.

Patrick blinked up at her from where he lay on the floor and let out a string of profanity.

A tap on the door behind told her Mandy was ready to return to the brunch.

"I suggest you clear the hall before Mrs. Crawford sees you. Your employer may not pay attention to my complaint, but he will hers." Abby slipped into the restroom.

Mandy smoothed her dress. "What happened out there?"

"Not much. I had a run-in with a guy who thinks too much of himself."

"It sounded like you floored him."

Abbie smiled. "You know it."

The hallway was empty when they returned to the banquet room.

Preston sat with Alan at Abbie's apartment, listening to the audio feed from Abbie's wire. He balled his fists and noticed Alan do the same. Patrick would never work within a thousand miles of Abbie again.

Alan started laughing at a thump followed by a string of expletives.

"What was that?"

"Patrick. My guess is he became victim to one of Abbie's signature moves. She has managed to drop every one of us to the floor with one of them, including Dad. I bet she has been waiting for years. I hope there was a security camera in the hall. I would enjoy watching her flip him repeatedly."

"You are telling me your sister flipped Patrick on his back? She is less than half his size."

Alan kept laughing. "And that, my friend, is the beauty of it. Her abilities are why I haven't been as uptight about the two of you as Adam and Alex are. I figure if you step out of line, she will take you out herself."

A text flashed on Alan's phone. "Dad says we will all meet here at eleven thirty. Crawfords are leaving the event early. Simon is coming."

Preston nodded and went back to the earlier conversation. "So, Adam and Alex don't like my hiring Abbie?"

"Pretty much. Alex has the twin thing going on and is always protective. Don't even try to figure it out. They had their own language until they were five. He used to try to protect her from us when they were little. Adam had a job like this go bad a few years ago when he got too close to a client. He doesn't want her hurt."

"I won't hurt her."

Alan looked Preston in the eye. "We don't always get to choose who we will hurt and who we won't."

The meeting took longer than it should to get started because Alan had gotten a copy of the security footage from the benefit. Preston wasn't sure if he should be proud or scared of his pretend fiancée. Jethro and Simon debated Patrick's fate for a while. In the end it was decided to let Patrick work in the hope that he would lead them to the stalker. Preston wanted to jail Patrick and be done with it. The Boston police would press charges.

Abbie doodled on a notepad. "We only have two weeks to find the stalker, and I don't know if we are any closer than we were before. There's got to be something we're missing."

"You're wrong. We know Patrick is involved." Alex's face hadn't changed from the grim expression he had worn since listening to the audio feed from Abbie's wire.

Abbie looked at Simon. "Is there some way you could wire him without him knowing?"

"Your father and I discussed that. But there are some legal issues. We have considered me 'hiring' someone on your father's team to be Patrick's new partner."

Adam stood near the window. "There is another option, and I want everyone to hear me out. Abbie needs to be more accessible. Living in a Hastings-secured building makes it harder for Patrick or the stalker to get to her. What if you do move into the guesthouse? We can put in some Hastings-controlled cameras and make it easier for the stalker."

"No." Everyone turned to stare at Preston. "Abbie was very clear on why she didn't want to move into the guesthouse. Things are going to be messy enough when we call off the engagement. I don't want Neanderthals like Patrick thinking she's easy." It irked him that Patrick thought he had inducted Abbie into the nonexistent club.

Next to him, Abbie sighed. "If it will help us find the stalker faster, maybe I should move in."

"Do you mind if we talk out on the balcony? And will you turn off any mikes you have out there?" Preston took her hand and led her outside.

Abbie looked over her shoulder. "We should have made them close the blinds, too."

Preston leaned on the railing. "When you refused to move in with me three weeks ago, I thought you were naive, but since then I have come to understand your point. I don't want you to compromise your values for this. Next week there are a few interviews scheduled with some of the local morning news shows. I want you to be able to show your purity ring and be just as proud of your accomplishment as you were the day you told me no."

"You never cease to amaze me, Preston. But this isn't about me. It's about a person who would scare a hundred people by planting a fake bomb. If we catch him this week, there won't be a next week or any interviews. Can you imagine what might happen if we don't find him and go to the fake-wedding phase? I can wear a gun under the dress, but not a bulletproof vest."

"Maybe we can get Mateo to sew in some Kevlar."

Abbie laughed. "And for the discerning, safety-conscious bride, we have the dress made to repel both insults and bullets."

Preston became serious. "How is the fake-wedding part going to work out for your reputation? After the break up it will be hard to get the media to separate the real you from the undercover you, because someone will figure it out."

"Not as bad as the news will for yours. Although the media has forgiven you for going through a half dozen serious girlfriends in three years. The people who know me will know the truth and that is what matters."

"I should call this off now. We can have Patrick arrested for planting the fake bomb and announce he was working with a stalker. Maybe the arrest will scare the stalker off."

"How about this: Let's give it another week. We can be out in public more and have a few parties at your house. Then we reevaluate. We can only wait so long before contacting the Boston PD about Patrick anyway." Abbie held out her hand for him to shake.

"Deal. With one exception. The first time this becomes life-threatening, it's over."

sixteen

HETEROCHROMIA. THERE WAS A BOY in the third grade with two different colored eyes and the teacher had put the word on their vocabulary test. Abbie looked at her reflection in the mirror. The transition between Abbie and Gale became harder each day as the lines between their personalities blurred. Each time she talked with Preston, she ended up sharing more of herself. The outsides looked different, but the interiors were meshing.

Abbie put in the other contact. Today she was to have tea with Margaret Harmon. Then there would be a party at the residence to celebrate the engagement. The stalker hadn't done anything since the bomb incident. Last night she had spent almost as much time waiting for the next attack as she had listening to the concert she'd attended with Preston and Felicia.

Her phone pinged. She didn't recognize the number.

Why don't you go away?

She picked up her other phone and called Alan. "Hey, I'm getting texts from a number I don't recognize."

"Probably a burner phone, but give me the number."

Abbie read off the number as another message came in.

You are not what he needs. A goody-two-shoes farm girl doesn't belong in our world.

"Listen to this text." Abbie read it emphasizing the words "our world." I think we are looking at someone from Chicago's 1 percent. Maybe some socialite Preston passed over."

"Simon ran checks on all the old girlfriends going back to the girl he married on the playground in first grade."

— Why can't I find your high school yearbook?

Abbie read the text to her brother. "Someone is trying to dig around. But homeschoolers like Gale don't have yearbooks."

— Are you going to answer me?

"I'll let you know if things escalate. But I need to finish getting ready."

"You do realize you didn't need to call me since we are monitoring your apartment? You only needed to yell at a camera."

"Um, maybe, but I am in my bathroom doing my makeup, and the cameras are off in here."

Alan laughed. "True, but you could have still yelled. The bedroom feed would have picked it up."

"Poor boy. If I call, you can't play with your toys. Goodbye, Alan."

Abbie was three minutes early to the restaurant. Margaret Harmon walked in the second the clock changed to 3:00 p.m. The tea proceeded as precisely as the etiquette book said it should. No one interrupted the meal, and nothing unusual occurred. Except Margaret showed she had a sense of humor. Abbie longed to tell her she would never be her daughter-in-law.

Margaret set down her teacup. "I am surprised you haven't changed the china pattern I picked out. It's absolutely hideous."

"I wondered if it wasn't some sort of test. I have picked another one, but I was trying to figure out the best way to change it and whether to tell you or not."

"Well, which one did you choose?"

"The Wedgwood Blue is my favorite, but I suspect there is already a set or four variations in the family collection. There is a red pattern I like, but I did want to make sure what I want doesn't duplicate anything."

Margaret smiled. "Common sense. I prayed my boy would find a woman with common sense. He won't appreciate your quality for years, but in a world where zeros start to become meaningless, common sense is the first penny to get lost."

They left the restaurant together. "Did you have your clothing sent to the residence for tonight's party?"

"I sent my dress with the driver."

Margaret linked arms with Abbie. "Then let's go change that hideous pattern and do a bit of shopping."

It turned out Margaret Harmon also had excellent taste in everything. And despite Preston's warning, she hadn't tried to change anything about the wedding. Abbie wondered how well Preston truly knew his mother.

Preston knocked on the door of the room Abbie was using to dress for the party. "Ready?"

Dressed in a robe, Abbie opened the door a few inches. "The stalker struck." She held up what could have been ruby-red party streamers, the only recognizable piece the bodice, where a heart shape had been removed.

"Your dress? What do we do?"

"Go find your mother. She'll have an idea."

Preston found his mother greeting guests and explained the problem. Mum disappeared through a side door. Less than ten minutes later, his mother escorted Abbie down the grand staircase. Preston maneuvered through the crowd to meet them both at the base.

"Where did you find a dress?"

His mother patted him on the shoulder. "Never ask a woman to reveal her sources. Now, you two go mingle."

Preston put his hand on the small of Abbie's back and started introducing her to the friends and family gathered to celebrate with them. Fortunately, this party was Mum's idea of small and only included around sixty people. Halfway through the introductions, after one of mother's friend's husbands insisted Abbie had been at a party last year, Preston realized why Abbie seemed to have no problem with so many people's names. She attended functions like this where she faded into the background as one of the nameless security personnel, sometimes obvious in a dark suit and at other times, like the New Year's party, where she was dressed to mingle. Most likely she already knew their names, their social situations, and probably who they hired for security.

Eventually, they made it to the dance floor, and Preston twirled her into a waltz. Abbie's face relaxed as she smiled up at him. "I am glad this was one of your mother's smaller parties. It helps to narrow down our list."

"What do you mean?" Preston spun her to the edge of the dancers, hoping no one would overhear.

"Whoever destroyed the dress did it in the hour before the party started. I checked on the dress when I returned with your mother. You and I talked for a moment, and I went to take a quick shower because the perfume girl at Sak's was a bit too aggressive. I locked the bedroom door when I showered, but the room was unlocked between the time I checked on the dress and my shower. Someone could have had a key and come in during my shower or come in earlier. So early arrivals, caterers, house staff. No one we talked to seemed to be overly shocked I would wear a vintage Dior dress. Although Felicia was a bit upset Margaret had loaned me something out of her collection when she wouldn't loan her anything. I pointed out the difference in sizes. This floor-length dress would drown your cousin. But then, she might have been upset someone had ruined my other dress. Felicia had picked the gown out when we were shopping the other day."

As Preston spun Abbie out and took a good look at the dress she now wore, a slightly faded photo came to mind. "Now I know where I've seen your dress. Mum wore it to her engagement party thirty-five years ago."

"Oh no." Abbie ducked her head.

"What?"

"Your mother likes me."

seventeen

THE FRIDAY MORNING MEETING WAS moved to Abbie's apartment so that she didn't need to go into the office. Both Simon and Preston were present by special invitation for the second half.

Referring to a paper in front of him, Jethro said, "The PIs finally tracked down the ex-model blogger. She changed her name and is living in Australia. She went on some TV fad diet and lost two-hundred pounds and is now their spokesperson. There is no evidence she knows Patrick or has ever tried to contact him, so she's off our list."

Simon sat next to her father. "I have heard from the Boston PD. The bomb was purchased from a Chicago-area prop shop. They would like to question Patrick and me again. They also would like to speak with Abbie and Preston. But with your wedding just a week away, they have agreed to send out a detective rather than ask us to go to Boston. He lands at O'Hare in an hour."

"My man has been able to find very little on Patrick this week, other than eliminating him from the dress cutting. Although he does suspect Patrick has more than one girlfriend. And not that it seems relevant to the investigation, but he did make two visits to the chiropractor this week. He threw his back out."

Adam and Alex high-fived Abbie. Everyone else clapped.

"If your father ever decides to let his secret weapon go, I'll double your pay." Simon's smile indicated he might be joking.

"Sorry, Simon. I'll stay with Dad. But back to the Boston PD. I think we should tell them what we believe. Eliminating Patrick from the stalker's resources will make her do more on her own." As Abbie shifted, her leg brushed Preston's, the contact setting her nerves on edge, probably because Alex sat on the other side of her glaring at Preston every two minutes.

Preston tapped his pen on his knee. "Her? You think the stalker is a woman?"

"From the texts I have been getting all week, yes. And the way the dress was cut, I am guessing female. And I think she did the dress personally. Why else cut a heart shape out of the bodice and keep it? The problem is Felicia had at least four friends at the residence from early afternoon on. And the caterer still can't account for two of the employees security counted. I think she is someone who wants the path clear so she can have a relationship with you." Who wouldn't? He'd proved he was one of the good guys, not to mention cute. Abbie hoped her thoughts didn't show. Her brothers would not be kind.

Preston rubbed his forehead. "If she is someone from my past, she probably has the money to hire almost anyone to do anything. But what you say indicates that she might be someone I've overlooked."

Jethro spoke. "As far as Patrick, I agree we should turn everything we know over to Boston PD. The fact we didn't report our suspicions a week ago could upset the detective, and we don't need an obstruction-of-justice charge."

"How many more events do you two have to attend?" asked Adam.

Abbie consulted her calendar. "Tonight's theater opening is the most public. Both Preston and I have shared our plans to be there on social media. And with the red-carpet walk, Dad already has extra security in place. Sunday afternoon I have the bridal shower. However, it's at Mandy's, and, as you know, Daniel is not overly happy and requested extra security. Tomorrow we are out on the lake, I think."

"We added as much extra security as we could for the bridal shower. Mom is coming out of retirement, and all the 'friends' we have added to the list are pros," said Alex.

"Next week, I have a final fitting, the rehearsal Thursday, and that night Candace is putting together a hen party."

Preston put his arm around her shoulder and leaned in to show her his calendar. "We have the family dinner on Monday and a private dinner at our favorite restaurant on Wednesday." He gave her a little squeeze. "Three of the Chicago-area morning shows have scheduled us for next week."

How could having his arm around her be both comforting and disconcerting? Next to her, she felt Alex tense. She hoped no one in the room was studying her too closely, as her heart rate had increased considerably. Abbie couldn't read the next item on her phone because her hand was shaking. She dropped both her hands and the phone to her lap, hoping no one had noticed. She couldn't accurately claim wedding jitters.

Simon consulted his watch. "I need to get out to O'Hare. I haven't told Patrick who's coming, but I assigned him to go with me to meet with an important guest this afternoon. Wish us luck. Preston, I'll text you where and when the detective wants to meet, if he does, after taking Patrick into custody."

As soon as the door shut behind Simon, Jethro stood. "I think we are done here."

Abbie turned to Preston. "Give me five minutes to grab my things."

She closed the door to her bedroom as well as the one to the bathroom, then cranked on the sink faucet and took several deep breaths. The ring on her finger twinkled in the light. Adam was right about the dangers of this job.

Jethro and Adam waited for the others to leave. Adam took a seat near the hallway leading to Abbie's room. Jethro took a place next to Preston. "We only have a minute. Abbie is going to be upset, but I am putting a tail on her. Adam is coordinating it. I called in a couple favors from old friends and got a few of their best to come in from New York and Dallas. Simon isn't to know." Jethro opened his phone. "Here are their photos. If they are as good as their bosses say, you shouldn't notice them. But you need to know so you don't hit your panic button."

"What if Abbie spots them?"

"Play it down and let Adam know."

Abbie came out of her room. "What is this? More threatening of the fake fiancé?"

Adam stood and put an arm around her shoulder. "We wouldn't do that."

"Liar." She tried to punch him, but he blocked her.

Jethro stood and hugged his daughter, then said something to her. Preston couldn't hear what they said. She hugged Adam too.

The door shut, leaving them alone in the apartment.

"Sometimes I am amazed they let me be alone in your apartment with you." Preston took his water glass into the kitchen.

Abbie pointed at three cameras. "Eyes and ears."

"Doesn't it freak you out knowing your family can see everything you do?"

"Only Alan sees much of it. Sometimes when I am alone, I talk to him. And I can turn off my phone. The bathroom only records if the system says I am out. There are some parts of my life I don't need an audience for." She smiled his favorite smile. "I also play jokes on them."

"Like what?"

"Make faces, chew with my mouth open. The other night after you left, I did the junior high thing where you hug yourself with your back to the camera. I've thought of stage kissing you to make Alex flip out."

"Stage kiss?" His curiosity took over.

Abbie took his face in her hands, slid her thumbs over his lips, kissed her thumbs, and stepped back.

An emptiness settled in Preston's center, something deep inside crying "No fair!" Not what he had imagined at all.

"Are they listening or watching now?"

Abby checked her phone. "Probably." She turned to one of the cameras. "You did catch that it was a stage kiss, right? All thumbs." She wiggled her thumb in front of the camera.

"Can you turn off the audio for a few? I want to talk to you."

Abbie nodded and tapped on her phone screen. Preston held out his hand. "Out on the balcony, so all they see is our backs."

Abby put her hand in his and followed him out. Preston didn't drop her hand when they reached the railing. "I noticed your hand shaking during the meeting. Tell me how you are doing."

She closed her eyes for a moment before answering. "I am worried about how this is going to affect people. Your mom let me wear her Dior. Your father thinks I can walk on water because I know starboard from port and pick up snakes. And you and I have become friends." She squeezed his hand.

More than friends. He didn't correct her.

"But we are so close. I think quitting now will bring even worse repercussions in your life. You can't ever be happy if you are worried about the woman you love being stalked. I've watched Daniel and Mandy live with the effects of the crazies who went after her. Even though there has only been one credible threat relating to Mandy since their wedding, Daniel still goes overboard with her protection sometimes. He finally learned to live normally, and then he realized he was going to be a dad, which, understandably, made him go overboard again. I know in the back of the minds of many people in your social circle is the need to protect children and grandchildren and spouses from crazies. But you shouldn't have to start a relationship off that way." Abbie stuck out her hand for a shake and deepened her voice. "Hi, my name is Preston. This is my bodyguard. Would you like to go on a date?"

Preston smiled at her joke. "There will always be the crazies and those who threaten to kidnap the family dog. And I am sure there will be other stalkers in the future who aren't afraid to make things dangerous."

"I know. Thanks to them, I make a pretty decent living. But this one has added stress to your life for three years. I suspect part of the tightness around your eyes has to do with #Prestoned and with how the media treats you like an uncaring, unemotional playboy who can't find the right trophy wife."

"Is that what you thought of me when you took the job?"

Abbie turned her head to look out over the lake. "Does it matter? I know I was wrong."

"Yes, it matters." The voice in the emptiness yelled at him to do something, but Preston wasn't sure what.

His phone beeped. "Simon wants us at the main office in half an hour."

"I'd better grab my real ID." Abbie went back into the apartment, leaving Preston alone with his thoughts.

eighteen

AMONG ALL THE COUPLES, THE single man holding a long-stemmed red rose in the theater lobby caught her attention. Abbie scanned the crowd and noticed three other men doing the same thing. She adjusted her grip on Preston's arm. "Something is wrong." She hit the panic button Simon had given her.

The first man stepped forward. "Gale 24? You promised to meet me here. What are you doing with him?"

The other men rushed over. "No, she promised to meet me."

"No, me. And I have the chat to prove it."

One man pulled out his phone. "This is what she promised me."

She caught a brief glimpse of a woman in lingerie.

"She said she'd go home with me." The first man threw a punch at the second.

Just as fast, two uniformed and two plainclothes security guards joined them. The bodyguard she recognized as Preston's skillfully separated Abbie and Preston from the rest.

"I want Simon to question them all," Preston said to the guard.

Five minutes later, Abbie and Preston waited outside an unused dressing room. Abbie typed a message to Adam.

I'm ok. Just give me 10 to figure this out. I'll put my phone on speaker during the interview.

— It's already on the news feeds. 'Men brawl over Preston's fiancée.'

She turned to Preston. "Does the media usually report things so quickly?"

"Only when they already happen to be there. I am assuming the photo the one guy flashed wasn't you."

"No. I have never been dressed like that in my life." Her cheeks grew warm at the thought.

Simon came down the hall. "Glad to see you two are unharmed. Never thought I would see your panic button light up. Glad I made you take it. By the way. Patrick didn't say anything more before leaving with the Boston detective. Let's see if these yahoos have anything to say before Chicago PD sticks their nose in."

Abbie and Preston followed Simon into the room. "Ok boys, this is how we are going to play this in the next five minutes. You answer questions, and I don't press charges when I turn you over to the boys in blue. Gale, ask away."

Abbie started with the first man. "Why did you call me Gale 24?"

"That is your profile name on HotDatesNow." The other men nodded. "Look at my phone if you don't believe me."

"I've never heard of this site. What is it?" Abbie took the offered phone.

One of the bodyguards cleared his throat and answered, "It is a pseudo escort service masquerading as a dating site."

Simon took one of the men's phones. "Decent manipulations, but they aren't you."

Abbie tried not to stare, but even she did a double take. "So, I agreed to meet all four of you here tonight?"

"Yes, you even sent my ticket for tonight to me after I paid my thousand dollars. I don't suppose I am getting my money back since I didn't get any action."

Preston growled. Her brothers were rubbing off on him.

Abbie touched his arm and shook her head. "When did I agree to our date?"

"Tuesday afternoon."

"Wednesday morning."

"2 am on Thursday after chatting with me for an hour."

"Wednesday evening."

"Well, gentlemen you have been set up. I suggest you cooperate with Mr. Dermot here. I am not a legal expert, but this sounds rather iffy. We can't protect you from the law if you were paying for services, but your cooperation will soften it. Now my fiancée and I are going to go enjoy the show." Abbie took Preston's arm and left the room.

   — **Alex just put his fist through the wall.**

   I think Preston wanted to put one through a face.

   — **Alan is already on the website doing his thing, so go enjoy the show.**

Abbie looked up from her phone at Preston. The concern in his eyes nearly invited her tears of frustration to come to the surface.

He pulled her into a hug. "You going to be all right?"

She nodded into his shoulder. "I just feel oddly dirty, like I am covered in slime. Who knows how many men saw that profile."

"Stalker. Not you. Let's go enjoy as much as we can."

At intermission, Abbie realized he'd never once let go of her hand, and she squeezed his. Someday she wanted a man who cared about her like this. If only this could be reality.

Saturday mornings were for sleeping in until at least seven, but Preston hadn't been able to sleep. Sometime during last night's show, a tabloid had discovered the fake Gale 24 profile. They'd left the theater by a back entrance before the curtain fell.

The stalker had gone after her reputation. It was also a blow to Preston's family.

Abbie texted. **We need to tell your parents.**

Abbie's text was more correct than she knew. Dad had wanted to call off the wedding last night because of the scandal. Mum had been near tears.

I'll set it up. Sending a car in an hour.

Breakfast in the gazebo was about as private as he could get. Once they were served, there would be no reason for any of the staff to linger. Both his parents had been up early and agreed to the meeting. Preston assumed they thought the meeting would end the relationship.

Abbie arrived with sunglasses on, which she refused to take off. On the walk out to the gazebo, she confirmed his thoughts. "I couldn't get the contacts in today. I guess I cried too much last night."

"How are your brothers dealing with this?"

"Alex came over last night." She didn't say more.

His parents waited at the gazebo. They all sat in silence while the staff served breakfast. As soon as they were alone, Abbie removed her glasses. Her blue eyes were rimmed with pink. She pulled her hair into a ponytail.

"Mr. and Mrs. Harmon, allow me to introduce myself: Abbie Hastings of Hastings security. I have been working with your son for the past month to put an end to the stalker who has been sabotaging your son's relationships for nearly three years. I can guarantee those photos are not of me, but that isn't the point of this meeting. The point is I have failed. The stalker is still working. Other than discovering she has been working with at least one member of your security team and narrowing the list of probable suspects, we have accomplished little. We have yet to stop her."

Preston jumped in before his father could speak. "This was my idea. I originally hired Abbie to guard Yvette before I proposed, but a billion little spiders ended our relationship, which was for the better. Since I already had things set up for a quick wedding, I asked Abbie to be my fake fiancée. I didn't realize at the time how complicated this would become. I figured we would catch the stalker in a week."

"Three years?" Mr. Harmon leaned on the table. "Someone has been stalking your girlfriends for three years, and you never told us? Why not? I thought you couldn't keep a woman."

"I thought I could handle the situation on my own. If it helps, all of them turned out to like the money more than they liked me." Preston took a drink of water so he didn't have to look his parents in the eye.

Mum studied Abbie. "So, you are not engaged?"

"He never even proposed. Just went down on one knee and put a ring on my finger. Everyone in the restaurant assumed." Abbie gave a little shrug.

"We have kept everything above reproach. The only time I kissed her was the night in the restaurant. Believe me, I knew those photos were fake the second I saw them."

Dad leaned back in his chair. "What do we do now?"

"There are two choices," Abbie began. "We call off everything. With the media showing blurred versions of the falsified photos, no one will blame him. Or we continue forward, hoping to catch the culprit so Preston can go choose himself a real bride without the stalker sabotaging her." Abbie's dispassionate layout of the options made the black hole in his heart grow.

"What happens if we get to Friday and you haven't caught her?" Mum asked.

"I could refuse to say 'I do' and run out of the wedding, or Preston has arranged for an actor to conduct the ceremony. We will forget to get our license until Friday morning, and I'll use a false name. All of which will invalidate the wedding. At the rate the stalker has been escalating, I doubt she will let me go on the honeymoon. Preston even joked about having the designer put Kevlar in the dress. Once she is caught, the story goes public. Preston loses much of his unearned reputation, and I go back to wearing dark suits and keeping someone else safe."

No one said anything for a moment. The food remained untouched.

Abbie broke the uncomfortable silence. "This is a family decision. Preston knows where to find me. She slipped off the ring.

I understand this is a family heirloom. I feel more comfortable leaving it here. Margaret, thank you for loaning me your Dior. I wish I had been worthy of it."

Preston wanted to go after Abbie as she left the table and crossed the lawn.

"Shame she isn't—" Mum took a drink of juice.

"She didn't say it, but if you call off the engagement now, she'll never get to salvage her reputation, and in black-and-white, those photos look like the real her." Mr. Harmon took a bite of his food.

Preston moved the fruit around his plate. "I know. I don't think she wants us to think about that."

They ate in silence.

"I think you should marry her." Mum's announcement caused a piece of muffin to get caught in Preston's throat. "I mean continue with the plan. Catching the stalker is the only option to bring everyone's lives back in order."

"I agree, son. Let's get this over with so we can move on. Seeing you went to a different security company, I suppose that means something?"

"Yes, only Simon knows, but that is how we realized Patrick Vonn was working with the stalker. Since he used to be on my team, it explains how the stalker accomplished some of the things she did. We are hoping that with a twenty-year sentence in Massachusetts for hoax bombs, Patrick starts talking. The Ritz could sue him as well."

"Will we be named in the suit?" asked Dad.

"I doubt it. I am a victim, as is Abbie. Plus, I paid the hotel a huge tip when we checked out early." Preston looked at his plate. He didn't remember finishing his eggs.

"I suppose I need to find a different gift for the shower. I bought a peignoir set I saw in Paris, and I'd like to give her something she can keep."

Preston nearly spit out his punch. His mother had bought a negligee for his fiancée? That was too weird. "Mum!"

"Oh, for heaven's sake. Many moms buy them for their daughters and leave the more risqué clothing for the bridesmaids to get. I figured since her mother was dead—that isn't true, is it? Mrs. Hastings isn't dead, is she?"

"No, and, in fact, she will be playing the role of Gale's aunt at the shower and at the wedding if necessary. I understand she is still a good shot and a retired bodyguard."

"She was an excellent shot back in the day. I'm glad you told me. I haven't seen her for years, but I might have recognized her and ruined everything. You don't think the stalker will try something there, do you?"

"Only if she's stupid. Mandy Crawford is hosting, and so Hastings Security is in charge. Not only do they have Mandy and her unborn baby to protect, but her brothers are all very upset Abbie is doing this. So far the stalker hasn't been willing to physically harm anyone beyond potential food poisoning, and doing anything where Mandy could get hurt will probably keep her at bay." Preston picked up the ring and put it in his breast pocket.

"The snake in the salad wasn't an accident?"

"Probably the stalker. Maybe paid someone in the kitchen." He stood and kissed his mother on the forehead.

"Oh."

His father caught his arm. "Tell her good luck from us. And when this is all over, she is still invited for a sail and to bring her family."

Preston walked into the residence. He didn't often spend time with his parents. He should make it a point to.

nineteen

MANDY LAY ON A DIFFERENT couch today. "I needed a different view. Candace and Zoe will be here in an hour, and my mother is baby shopping again. I shouldn't encourage her, but it's better than her hovering."

Abbie took a seat on the floor so she could be eye level with her friend. "Have you seen the news?"

"Yes, and for the record, whoever manipulated those photos did an abysmal job. Anyone with half a brain can see they are spoofed."

Abbie tried to smile. "I guess I'm lucky they didn't hire you."

"You know I don't do that type of work. I see the ring is gone. Is the job over? I was looking forward to the shower tomorrow."

"You do realize that even if the shower is still on, I am returning all the gifts, right?" Abbie pulled her knees up to her chin. "We met with Preston's parents this morning." She bit her lip and blinked. "They are going to decide what to do. This is so stupid. It shouldn't feel like we are really breaking up, but my ring finger feels naked, and my heart—"

Mandy reached out. "Scoot closer so I can hug you."

Abbie leaned against the couch, and Mandy gave her a half hug.

"When did you realize you loved him?"

"I don't know. I didn't fall in a day. I started out not even respecting him. But if I had to name a moment, it would be the afternoon he tried to convince me I was beautiful. But I *knew* when I saw the bomb and I needed him safe. He gave me chances to back out since then, but I couldn't. I can't leave him to keep going through this until he finds a woman who is desperate enough to have a backbone or who loves him—"

Mandy gave her another hug. "Should I text Candace to bring ice cream back for us?"

"I don't think ice cream can solve this one. Besides, the fewer people who know, the easier this will be."

"Ice cream doesn't solve problems, but it only freezes the pain."

Abbie leaned against the couch. "I can't decide if I want to finish this job or not. If we don't catch her and I have to stand up in front of a fake minister and say I do, I don't know how I will survive. And the worst part is I can't let him know because he can't marry his bodyguard. I'm just the staff."

"You are not just the staff. You never have been."

"That is a problem too. You know I can't be your regular bodyguard after the baby comes. I have lost my objectivity."

Mandy patted Abbie's shoulder. "I've known for a while. That's why I offered you two paid months off after she shows up. I'd rather have you as my friend anyway. But I still want you at the hospital. No way are any of your brothers coming into the delivery room."

Abbie laughed. "You do realize nothing is going to happen in the delivery room, and even if my brothers were there, they would be outside the door, right?"

"I know." Mandy rubbed her belly. "I guess I finally understand why Daniel goes from normal to overprotective in half a heartbeat."

Abbie's phone pinged. "It's Alex. Preston is at my apartment looking for me."

"Go in my bathroom and use whatever you need to put your face back on. Also, lose the ponytail. And text me after, okay?"

Abbie nodded and prepared to meet the verdict.

Alex set his phone down. "She is at Mandy's. Give her fifteen minutes."

Preston grabbed a water and sat on the couch. "Are you going to sit here and glare at me the entire time?"

"You know she cried most of the night, don't you? She works in a tough world with even tougher men. Patrick isn't the only jerk who has made inappropriate remarks or advances. A couple men found Gale's phone number and texted asking if they could sign up for her side business too."

"She didn't tell me."

"Adam took care of it. Most of those in our line of work know her well enough to know the photo wasn't her, but I think she is worried about this when the real Abbie comes back." Alex sat down on the chair opposite Preston. "I hope you are going to do your best to fix this mess for her."

"Of course I will. Don't think I liked seeing her red-rimmed eyes any more than you did. I didn't have the luxury of putting my fist through a wall."

"Nah, you have the luxury, just not the muscles." Alex's smile was no less threatening than his glare.

"Maybe."

They both drank their waters. Preston wondered who would out-glare the other.

"Adam warned her not to take this job. Told her the stakes were too high. Too easy to blur the lines between personal and professional. Since you're here, I'm assuming you are going to continue this week. There are going to be a lot of talk-show hosts and others who are going to shout for you to kiss her. I don't care what she says. Her emotions are involved, and those endorphins from kissing will only mess with her mind. Know that every time you cross that line, I will keep track, and I will get you in a sparring ring somehow, and you will pay a punch per kiss. Break her heart and it's a full ten minutes."

"I don't want to hurt her. Your sister is one of the closest friends I have had in a while. I don't know if it makes it harder or not knowing that. If I do kiss her, I'll step into the ring and let you pound away. A punch for every kiss other than the one in front of the minster. I don't see a way out of that."

"Deal."

Preston knew it would be bone crushing, but he stood and shook the man's hand anyway.

"Looks like I got here in time. No wrestling in the apartment." Abbie closed the door and took off her sunglasses. "Alex, if you don't mind going elsewhere? And FYI, I am turning off the cameras and audio. If they are not back on in a half hour, feel free to come back."

Alex gave his sister a questioning look but left. Abbie punched some buttons on her phone. "I hope you don't mind, but I wanted us to be able to speak freely."

"Thanks. I'm glad." Preston fished the ring out of his front pocket. "As Dad pointed out, the only way to clear your reputation is to catch the stalker, and you've done too much work to let this go. Let's finish this together."

He slipped the ring on her finger.

"How did your parents take it?"

"Mum went to find a new gift for the shower tomorrow. She wanted something you can keep, and the gift she purchased in Paris was…inappropriate." Preston felt heat rise in his face.

"Are you blushing? Oh my. I'm glad she is not giving me whatever it was."

Preston drank more water.

"So, what are we supposed to do this afternoon? I need to put my eyes in and get ready."

"Sailing, but we can do something else."

Abbie looked out her window. "Have you ever been to the Navy Pier?"

"Not for at least a decade."

"Let's get you a T-shirt so you don't stand out and go have some fun!"

"I'll go get one while you get ready." Preston headed for the door.

Abbie followed him. "Try one of the souvenir shops a block over."

twenty

ABBIE REREAD THE TEXT MESSAGE from the new unknown number.

Miss Purity Ring joined the mile-high club and is upset about my dating prank. Hypocrite.

"Guys, are you listening in?"

"What is it, Abbie?" Alan's voice came from the stereo speaker.

"She may have talked with Patrick." She read the text. "Check with Boston PD and see who he's communicated with. Oh, and she is using a new number again."

"What's on your agenda today?"

"Interview for the 11:00 a.m. news broadcast, last fitting, and dinner with the family at the mansion. Oh, and tell Dad I spotted his tails again yesterday. So if they are not his, he needs to fess up."

Jethro's voice came over the speaker. "I knew I trained you well. But live with them for the rest of the week."

"Only for you, Dad." She bent over to slip on her heels. "Love you."

A girl shouldn't have the final fitting for her wedding dress alone, but Abbie couldn't endure the festive atmosphere her bridesmaids would bring with them.

At the beginning of her junior year of high school, she'd found a copy of a bride magazine in the recycle bin of the library. When

Alex hadn't been looking, she'd stuffed it in her backpack. She'd kept the magazine in the bottom of her feminine-items drawer so none of her brothers would ever find it. Between the ad for silver and the tux ad with the redhead, there was a dress she'd fallen in love with. But the magazine was only a memory, and her former dress crush was long out of style. Looking in the mirror, Abbie fell in love with a new dress.

She spoke to her reflection. "It's beautiful. I look—"

"Gorgeous, just like I knew you would."

Abbie turned to the doorway where Preston stood. "You are not supposed to be in here. It's bad luck to see the bride in her dress before the wedding."

"Only if you believe that sort of thing. But you didn't bring any of your friends, and I don't think a bride should be alone at her last fitting."

The designer came back into the room with the veil. "Mr. Harmon, I didn't expect you here."

"Sorry, Mateo. I couldn't wait to see your creation for her."

Abbie bent down so the veil could be put into place.

"You should get a new color job before the wedding. You don't want your roots to show. Also, wear your hair up and lose the extensions." Mateo adjusted the veil and turned to Preston. "With her hair up, some diamond-drop earrings would complete the look. Not too big—maybe two to three carats total, and platinum, not gold."

Preston strolled around the pedestal. "Thank you for your recommendations. Will you give us a minute?"

The designer sauntered off.

"You have no idea how picture-perfect you look, do you?"

The mirror confirmed her fears. She was blushing. "Is this your way of turning me into a blushing bride?"

"No, it's my way of telling the truth."

Abbie turned away from his appreciative gaze and blinked back the tears that formed. Preston handed her a handkerchief.

"I didn't think anyone carried these anymore." She mopped at the tears.

"Tell me why you are crying."

"Wedding jitters?"

"Pardon me if I don't believe you." He walked back into her line of sight and reached for her hand. "Abbie?"

"Any woman would cry seeing herself in a dress like this. It's one of those woman-hormone things men always complain about."

"Is that a question or a statement?"

Abbie blinked back the last tear. "Both?"

Preston laughed.

Abbie swiped at his shoulder. "I'd better get out of this dress. We have a TV studio to get to."

"Let me give you a hand down."

Abby hurried to the dressing room. She wasn't sure, but she thought she heard him call her beautiful. The story about not wearing makeup on the bride's wedding day made more sense.

Green rooms were never green. The fact had bothered Preston since he first stepped into one with his grandmother as a young teen. Abbie was still in makeup when the producer came in.

"Mr. Harmon, thank you for coming. Janet will ask you the standard questions—How did you meet, future, etc."

"That's what she told my assistant. Ten-minute session, I believe." Preston handed the producer the faxed copy of the questions. "My lawyers approved all but question number three. Gale's parents' deaths is a no go."

The producer took the list and turned to leave, then stopped. "Are you willing to kiss on camera?"

"Absolutely not."

An arm slipped through his. "My fiancée means that as a courtesy to me. He has agreed to no public kissing until the wedding."

"Miss Henderson, nice to meet you. I'm the producer. I'll be back with someone to put your mikes on." The man hurried away.

Preston turned to Abbie. "I didn't realize you were a diplomat."

"I'm sure there are several things you don't know about me." Abbie smiled at him.

He wished he had a lifetime to find them all out.

The sound technician helped them get in their mikes and tested them. The producer returned. "We are about to go to a commercial break. If you will follow me."

Preston gave Abbie's hand a squeeze. "Nervous?"

She rolled her eyes at him.

Iconic hostess Janet conferred with the producer. Preston saw him pass the reviewed copy of the questions to her. The audience consisted of only about sixty people, enough to provide live clapping.

The producer ran off stage, and someone counted them down.

"Welcome back, Chicago. This is the segment you have all been waiting for: Monday Marriages. Let me be the first to introduce you to Chicagoland's favorite couple, Preston Harmon and Gale Henderson." The crowd cheered.

The questions followed the approved outline.

"Most of our Monday Marriage couples kiss at the end of the segment. But I understand you two declined to do so. Any reason for this?"

Abbie answered. "Our first kiss ended up all over social media. I felt this cheapened our relationship. I wasn't used to the attention. Preston promised me there would be no more public kissing until the wedding."

"I don't understand how you of all people could feel that way when you posted those revealing photos on the HotDatesNow website. According to Preston's ex-girlfriend, Yvette, he proposed to you less than 120 hours after he proposed to her. Did you not, in fact, meet Preston through your Gale24 web page?"

Images of the web page filled the screen behind them. Preston tried to jump up, but Abbie held him down. "Preston did not find me through that site. If you had done your due diligence, you would see that the page you are showing was created eight days ago. And any member of your graphics department would tell you the photos are manipulated."

She let go of Preston's leg, and he jumped up, bringing Abbie with him. "I believe our interview is over."

In the green room he ripped off his mike and helped Abbie remove hers. The producer tried to cut them off as they left, but Preston's bodyguard was faster at getting them out of the room.

"Mr. Harmon! Mr. Harmon!" the producer yelled after them.

As soon as they reached the car, Preston called his lawyer on speed dial. "Gordon, they overstepped. The last question was about the website."

"I'm already on it."

"Thanks."

He turned to Abbie. "Do you want me to cancel the others?"

"Can I just have a hug?"

Preston wished he had thought of that first.

twenty-one

ABBIE REACHED IN TO TURN on the light in her apartment. Odd. The entry light should have turned on when she unlocked the door. She stepped back into the hall and slipped her Glock out of her thigh holster, then reached for her phone, tapping the button that set off her panic notification.

Adam burst out of the stairwell, gun drawn. Abbie stayed in place until he reached her and whispered, "The apartment feed went dark seven minutes ago. We can't get the electric online."

The elevator pinged. A building-security member and one of the bodyguards who had been following her for three days got off.

Adam took charge. "Meet Peter. Go with Peter."

"But—"

"If someone is in there, you don't need to be seen."

Abbie followed Peter into the elevator. "Nice to meet you officially." She stuck out her hand.

"Do ya want to put your Glock away before we reach the lobby?"

Abby turned her back to him, slipped her gun back into the holster, and fixed her skirt. "You must be the one from Texas."

"Yes, ma'am."

They crossed the lobby to the guardroom. One guard was on his headset, another on the computer, a third monitoring the screens. The first turned to her, headset in hand. "Your brother wants to talk with you."

"Thanks." She held the headset to her ear. "What did you get?"

"It's all clear. As soon as we get lights up in here, I'll need you to come up. And I hope you didn't spend all your clothing budget. Oh, and why didn't Preston walk you up?"

Abbie didn't want to answer. "The dinner at the mansion didn't go well. Today's TV appearance and the lawyers had the family on edge. It turned into a feud. A couple people even walked out. I told Preston to stay there and see if he could calm things down, and came back alone."

"We have light. Bring Peter with you."

Abbie stepped around the broken glass in the kitchen. The sofa had been slashed. "Ready to see the bedroom?" Alan came out with a camera around his neck. Abbie tried to step around her brother, but Alan stopped her. "It's ketchup."

Even having been warned, the blood-red words on the bed still caused her to stop. The clothes were slashed, top half on the hangers, bottom half on the floor. Her Canon was shattered in a thousand pieces on the bathroom tile.

Adam came out of the bathroom. "Looks like she took your butcher knife and sliced through them in a couple strokes. Quick and angry. She also left a high end set of night vision goggles in the kitchen. Maybe we can get some DNA or finger prints."

"How did she get the lights off?"

"Still working on that. Best guess is she found the breaker to the apartment. A master electrician will be here in an hour."

"Hallway cameras?"

Alan stuck his head in the room. "Morph suit again."

"We should report this to the police, shouldn't we?" Abbie folded her arms.

Adam pulled her into a half hug. "A detective is on his way. You need to let Preston know."

Two aspirin probably wouldn't touch the headache, but Preston downed them anyway. The dinner had been a disaster. Why had Felicia started in on Abbie in the first place and then stalked out? Thankfully Mum and Dad hadn't budged, but Abbie had still left before the dessert was served. She was right. Tempers had calmed once she'd departed.

He needed to call her.

Dead phone. Maybe seeing her in the dress before the wedding was a mistake.

He plugged the phone in and gave it a minute to spring back to life.

Seven missed calls. Three from Abbie.

Preston didn't bother listening to the voice messages. He dialed her number.

"Preston?"

"Did I wake you? Your voice sounds—"

"Tired. Did you listen to my voicemails?"

"No, I realized my phone had died during dinner and saw your calls and one from Alan. What's wrong?"

"My apartment was vandalized. It was bad enough we had to call the police. I told them about some of it, as they already knew about the website and opening-night mess. I wanted you to know before some reporter gets wind of this." Something in her voice gave him pause.

"Have you been crying?"

"No, I'm just frustrated. She only had seven minutes before I got there. She ruined every piece of clothing I had in the closet. Thank goodness I had the dress delivered to Mandy's and I returned your mom's Dior. The couch, the bed, the mirror, the dishes. It looked like the Tasmanian Devil had been through there."

Preston put back on his shoes. "Where are you now? I'm coming over."

"I checked into a hotel. I'll text you which one in the morning. Adam is in the adjoining room, so I am safe."

"So I'll see you at seven?"

"Yes, but be warned. My wardrobe is rather limited."

"How limited?" Preston removed his shoes.

"I still have everything I wore to dinner tonight and an old set of sweats from Adam's go-bag. But I think the sweats are not the thing for the morning show. I keep one of my business suits at Mandy's, so I have four options. Most of my personal clothes are too casual or in Indiana."

Preston thought of the clothes in the sample room of their premier fashion magazine. "Actually, I think I know where to get you a few things before seven in the morning. Do you have shoes?"

"Only the ones I wore tonight. She dumped most of them in my tub and ran the water. I haven't seen what is salvageable." Abbie yawned.

"Try to get some sleep , and I'll see you in the morning."

"Thanks, Preston. Good night to you too."

twenty-two

"You look like death warmed over."

Abbie put in the second contact. "Wow. Thanks, brother. Just what every girl needs to hear an hour and a half before she goes on TV." She pushed Adam out of the doorway and closed the bathroom door. The makeup team at this morning's station better be top-notch. Mateo was right. Her roots were showing. Hopefully spray color could cover them for the next couple days.

Abby twirled a strawberry lock around her finger. If getting her hair done regularly didn't take so much time, she would be tempted to keep it this way. It had been fun wearing her hair down and dressing up this month. She would need to add a few more skirts and dresses to her wardrobe. If only the stalker hadn't slashed her collection—there were three she especially liked, but they were out of her normal budget.

Adam knocked on the bathroom door. "Preston is here with clothes."

Anything would be better than the oversized sweats. Preston stood next to the bed where a pile of clothing lay. He stepped forward and held her by the upper arms. "You didn't sleep well, did you?" He pulled her into a hug. "I'm so sorry Abbie, I should have never—"

Abbie shook her head but stayed in the hug. Behind them, Adam cleared his throat. Abbie stepped back. "What do you think about going public with the stalker? My brothers think the publicity might help."

Preston didn't look at Adam, and he didn't release her hands. "What do you think?"

"It can't hurt. Sometimes hiding a problem only magnifies it. Also, if we mention the stalker this morning, we can beat any two-bit journalist hanging around their police scanners. Alan has some photos of last night's damage, and most of the city has already seen the falsified photos of me. Pointing out they are fakes may help that story die. Who knows? Someone may know something and not realize it."

"While you get dressed, I'll call the producer and let him know about the change. I'll also call the lawyer. After yesterday, no show is going to go off script without written approval."

Abbie looked at the clothes on the bed. "Where did you find these?"

"I raided the sample room of one of the fashion magazines. After we are done with the interview, I'll take you shopping and we can pick up a few new things for you. Most of the clothes on the bed need to go back to where they came from." Preston followed Adam into the adjoining room and closed the door.

Abbie sorted through the clothes. The pale-blue sundress with its embroidered floral jacket looked particularly cheerful, which was just what she needed.

Adam accompanied them to the studio claiming no one would think anything of an extra bodyguard. Preston spent most of the ride talking to his lawyer, who finally agreed to come down to the set.

Abbie was whisked into hair and makeup. The makeup artist frowned a little. "Wedding jitters keeping you up? Don't worry. I am used to covering up the too-early-in-the-morning look, which is much easier than the hung-over face some people show up with."

Fifteen minutes later, the transformation was complete. Abbie studied her reflection. "You're sure those are makeup brushes and not magic wands?"

The makeup artist laughed. "No, they are just regular brushes. Now go conquer the world."

In the green room, which did have green couches, Abbie met Gordon, the lawyer, and the producer. Adam had left while she was still in makeup, having been replaced by other guards.

Preston took Abbie by the hand and walked her over to the far side of the room. "Are you sure about this?"

Abbie nodded, remembering not to bite her newly glossed lips.

"I wish—" Preston was interrupted by the sound technician and changed whatever he was going to say. "By the way, you look fantastic. I hope the dress is not one that needs to go back to where it came from. If it is, I'll buy you one like it."

"Thanks."

The producer led them onstage.

The interview went according to the script. Preston had been interviewed by Michelle before and hoped for nothing less.

"Yesterday one of our rival stations showed some photos they claim to have received from an anonymous source. Our station also received them, but I understand this incident is one of many. Preston, is it true you have a stalker who is out to destroy your love life?"

"For the past three years, my girlfriends have been scared away by what both my security team and the Chicago PD believe to be the same stalker. The closer I come to the altar, the more the stalker escalates. Unfortunately, Gale has been on the receiving end of the stalker's worst escapades yet. A week and a half ago, with the help of a hired man, she planted a faux bomb at the Boston Ritz." Images from a Boston affiliate station played on the screen behind them. "Then the stalker created a fake profile for Gale on one of the more notorious dating websites. The profile was removed with the help of the Chicago PD. However, the stalker duped several news outlets into reporting this profile as newsworthy."

The talk-show host directed the next question to Abbie. "Have there been other incidents?"

"A few mostly harmless things: black roses, nasty texts, a little green snake in my salad." The audience gasped. "He was probably more scared than the rest of my table mates and has been safely returned to his natural habitat."

"So why are you going public with this now?" asked Michelle.

Preston answered. "Last night Gale returned to her apartment to find this." Photos of the apartment filled the screen. "The words on her bed, which are blurred out, thank you, are written in ketchup, not blood, but they still constitute a death threat."

"Gale, what did you think when you saw this?"

"I was in shock. Even this morning I can't understand the type of rage that would destroy almost everything I had in less than seven minutes, according to building security."

A photo of Abbie's closet filled the screen. Michelle gave the camera a wide-eyed stare. "Every woman out there is probably as shocked as I am to see this closet. Did she destroy everything?"

"I think most of the clothes I had were damaged in some way. I had to borrow a dress for the show this morning."

"I don't see a wedding dress in these photos. Please tell us it's safe."

Preston smiled at Abbie, she amazed him. "Gale's wedding gown was spared as it was not at the apartment, but my bride would look just as gorgeous if she had to grab something off the rack this morning to replace the gown Mateo designed for her."

The audience gave a collective sigh. Abbie blushed.

"If you think you know something about Preston and Gale's stalker, please contact the Chicago PD. Preston and Gale, thank you for being in our studio, and we wish you felicitations on your wedding this Friday."

The mood in the green room was festive. The producer hurried in. "Thank you, Mr. Harmon, Miss Henderson." He turned to the lawyer. "Is the segment good to go? I'd like to air the interview in ten."

The lawyer waited for Preston's nod before signing off on the segment.

Preston took Abbie's hand. The action had become natural over the past few weeks. "Breakfast, then shopping?"

"I don't need much—just a couple outfits."

"I know, but shopping could be fun. We could make a game of it."

"Like find a dress to match your ugly tie?" Abbie waited for the driver to open the door.

Preston straitened his tie. "It is not ugly."

Abbie laughed.

The lawyer hurried up to them. "Mr. Harmon, a moment." Gordon dropped his voice. "You haven't asked us to write a prenup, and the wedding is only three days away. I need to meet with her lawyers."

A prenup had never crossed his mind, not for a fake marriage.

Abbie took his arm. "Gordon, or is it Mr. Gordon? Let's make this easy. If I get a divorce, I may only keep my clothing as Preston won't need my skirts or heels. I am not marrying Preston for his money. If he chooses to give me anything more, it will be his choice. I will return the ring as it's a Harmon family heirloom. Does that work for you?"

"What about children?" asked Gordon.

"Mr. Gordon, do you think Preston is an honorable man? I do. I will trust if we have children he will not let them go hungry or ignore their needs. If you need that in writing, I'm sure you can draft it."

"Miss Henderson, it's standard for the bride to ask for several million dollars plus alimony."

"My mother taught me to never plan on a divorce. If our marriage fails, I don't want Preston's money." Abbie slipped into the car.

"Sir, is that what you want me to write up? She gets nothing?" Gordon raised his brows in disbelief.

"Put some legalese in there to the effect that if I choose to give her a settlement, she can't return the money."

"Are you kidding, sir?"

"Nope." Preston got in the car, shut the door, and closed the window between them and the driver.

"Sorry if I embarrassed you in front of the lawyer, but I don't want there to be any questions if we are still looking for her on Friday."

"Hypothetically, if this were all real, would you have asked for anything different?" Preston wanted to know if he was right.

"No, when I get married, it's with the mind-set of celebrating my fiftieth and even seventy-fifth anniversaries with him. I don't expect everything will be easy and hearts and flowers. Money or no money, making a good marriage is hard work. I don't think having tons of money if the marriage fails will make me feel any better. If there are children, I hope I chose wisely enough that he would still support them. If not I have a career and a family that will support us."

"You could take a nice vacation with the money."

"Okay, call Gordon and add an all-expense-paid, two-week vacation to Bora-Bora." Abbie rolled her eyes and laughed.

Preston looked out the window and hoped they would get to the restaurant soon. He was very much in danger of pulling her into his arms and kissing her.

twenty-three

IF SHE HADN'T SEEN THE damage to the apartment, she would never have believed it. The smell of new paint and carpet lingered under the lavender air freshener. But otherwise, everything was in the same place. Abbie opened the empty closet. Well, almost everything. The three pieces of clothing that hadn't been slashed were with forensics.

She opened her bags from today's shopping trip. She had won the find-a-dress-to-match-the-tie game as Preston didn't wear the same tie two days in a row. In the end, she convinced Preston she only needed four outfits for the rest of the week. After all, the black dress and a pale-green suit had been at the cleaners and spared. Shopping with him was fun. He would find something off the bargain rack and pair it with something outrageously expensive to see the look of shock on her face when she saw the price tags.

Her phone pinged. Preston.

— Gordon says he has the papers drawn up and we can get them in the morning after the show.

Sounds good. Don't do anything too crazy tonight.

— Don't worry. I won't have a hangover in the morning.

Preston's bachelor party. She doubted if any of his friends would be too upset to find out they'd celebrated for nothing.

Abbie thought of going to Mandy's, but she wanted to be alone. The hen party was planned for Thursday, the knowledge that the get-together would be a how-do-we-distract-Mandy party was the only reason she hadn't canceled it.

Her phone double beeped. The doorman. "A woman claiming she is your Aunt Betty is here to see you."

"Can I see her on video, please?" *Mom.* "Please send Aunt Betty up."

Abbie hung up the last of the clothing and went to answer the door. As soon as the door closed, she hugged her mother. "Why are you here?"

"My baby girl is getting married in three days. I came to give her 'the talk.'"

"Mom!"

Melanie Hastings laughed. "Don't look so shocked. But do whatever you need to so your brothers don't hear us."

The stereo speaker popped once before Alan spoke. "Leave the video on and know that if the feed goes dark, someone will be there in under forty-five seconds."

"Do they do that often?" Mom set a takeout bag on the counter.

Abbie punched the code in the phone. "Not too often, but this much surveillance brings the "Good night John Boy" routine to a whole new level. Which reminds me—if you need to use the bathroom, there is a button under the counter by the door. Push it to stop and start the video feed. They want the camera on 24/7 now."

Mom pulled out a couple plates. "I would have brought my chicken and dumplings, but I didn't know what the guard would do with homemade, so it's Orange Chicken and Crab Rangoon."

"So why did you come?" Abbie scooped some rice out of a box.

"Because you are about to make a more colossal mistake than any of your brothers ever did. And someone needs to stop you."

"Bigger than trying to row across Lake Michigan?"

"Adam was only ten. Doesn't count."

Abbie pulled apart a wanton. "How about bigger than naming your children with all *A* names?"

"At least I alphabetized you. And I only regret your names in moments of rage. Do you have any water?"

"Poor Andrew thought his name was Adam-Alan-Alex-No-Andrew until he was five." Abbie got water out of the fridge.

"Stop changing the subject. This is your mistake we are talking about."

"What mistake?"

"You aren't marrying the right man."

"I'm not marrying anyone."

"That's the problem. You should be marrying Preston, and I am not talking about a wedding with some actor officiating so you can catch this anti-cupid culprit."

"Mom, out of the question. I can't go up to Preston and tell him I want this to be real."

"Why not?"

"For one, he is my client. Two, his name is on *Fortune*'s list. And three, he is Preston Harmon."

"Are you saying you're not good enough because he's rich?"

"No, I am not saying that. I am saying a relationship isn't possible. He is a wonderful employer, but in the end, I am still just staff."

"Not the way he looks at you."

Abbie set down her chopsticks. "How do you know how he looks at me?"

"TV."

"Interviews don't count. Acting time."

Mom got up and walked into the living room. She turned to the corner and gave a thumbs up. "Not that TV. This one."

Clips from the last four weeks filled the screen. Mom put her hand up, and the film stopped. "Up to this point, he has looked at you as an interesting female. But look at him in this meeting." She started the video with a wave of her hand. "There. Genuine concern."

"So Preston is concerned."

"Keep watching. Here he has moved into protective mode."

Abbie put her hand up, but the video didn't stop. "Mom. Please, no more. I know what happens next. It's better I keep telling myself it's only my imagination."

The video continued.

Abbie ran for the bathroom, closed the door, and hit the Off button before the first tear could escape.

The last talk show was the easiest. No surprises. No trick questions. Abbie teared up a bit when the host showed how much support they were getting from the social media world. But she had been silent since they'd left the stage. The driver held the door open, and they got in the car.

Preston held her hand. "Is something wrong?"

"Just worried because the stalker was silent yesterday. Maybe I should have let you put Kevlar in the dress." Her smile didn't reach her eyes.

"We have a couple stops to make. My parents want to meet us for lunch."

Abbie closed her eyes for a long minute. Preston squeezed her hand.

"I'm fine. I want her to strike now. If she waits until the wedding. I don't think an attack will be a hoax this time."

"Let's pray it doesn't get to that."

"I've been praying all month."

The car pulled up in front of an office building. Preston exited first and helped Abbie out. Gordon's secretary let them into a conference room. Gordon entered with an older lawyer Preston recognized as Gordon's father.

"Mr. Harmon, Miss Henderson, take a seat. This is my father, Mr. Jacobson. We prepared the agreement according to your specifications. Please take your time to review these. Miss Henderson, where is your attorney?"

"I don't have one."

The elder Mr. Jacobson sat down. "This is highly unusual."

Abbie looked over the paper. "Because I am asking for nothing or because I have no lawyer? Or—" She paused for a moment. "Or is it this line Preston must have asked you to put in about me not being able to return his gifts?" She ran her pen through the section. "I'd like these lines struck before I sign." She pushed her paper across the table to Gordon.

This will take a moment. "Preston, is this acceptable to you?"

"Not particularly, but I can't force Gale to take a gift she doesn't want." He should have talked to her about the clause. Maybe when this was all over, they could renegotiate. She would be signing under a false identity anyway.

Gordon returned with new papers. Abbie scribbled across the bottom of the page. Preston took the sheet and signed on his line before handing the page to Gordon.

Gordon took the paper. "I'll have copies delivered to both of you."

Abbie took Preston's hand in the elevator on the way down. "Thanks for trying to put in the gift line. But you knew I wouldn't agree."

"You can't blame a guy for trying."

"No, I can't, and the gesture was sweet."

They reached the car and got in. "No one other than my grandmother has ever called me sweet."

"Well, then, I must have found your secret."

The car stopped, and they climbed out.

Abbie stopped before clearing the door. "City hall?"

Preston turned to the driver. "This isn't on this morning's list."

The driver held up his phone. "Your assistant put it on the schedule. You have an eleven-thirty appointment."

Consulting his schedule, Preston discovered the driver was correct. He pressed a button and called his assistant. "Max, how did the appointment get on my schedule?"

"Mrs. Margaret called during your TV interview this morning. She said you had forgotten to include getting your license and asked me to make an appointment. I got the last slot of the week, unless you want to stand in the general line, which can take up to three hours."

"Thanks, Max." Preston put his phone back in his pocket and held his hand out for Abbie. "Mum wanted to make sure this was on our schedule." He could talk to Mum later.

Abbie didn't speak until they were nearly to the building. "What about our plan to get the license Friday so it's invalid without the twenty-four-hour waiting period?"

"Apparently that involves a three-hour wait in line."

At the office, Abbie stopped suddenly, Preston nearly tripping when the firm grip on his arm stopped him too. He turned to face her.

Abbie searched in her purse and looked up, eyes wide. "I only have my real ID."

It took a moment for Preston to realize what she was saying. "If the license is never witnessed and turned in, it won't be valid, and we still have the actor. No worries."

He escorted her into the office. The appointment was over quickly. The clerk signed the certificate and slipped it in an envelope. "Congratulations. Have a happy wedding."

Preston handed the license to Abbie. "Souvenir."

twenty-four

ABBIE CHECKED THE MIRROR ONE last time and looked in the closet where the black dress from their first date hung. The deep-green dress Preston bought her yesterday was specifically for this date. Their last.

Before turning out the light in her bedroom, she looked up into the camera. "Pray she strikes tonight, guys."

The stereo popped. "A two-edged prayer, pumpkin. Keep your eyes open."

"I will, Dad."

Preston knocked at the door. Abbie opened it to find him with a dozen roses and a bag. "I brought a vase this time."

"Come in. I'll put them in water."

Preston followed her into the kitchen and set the bag on the counter, then pulled the vase out.

She recognized the vase from her china shopping trip with Margaret. "Where did you get this vase?"

"Just around."

"I think you know exactly where you got it. But I am going to say thank you and hope I can find a place my brothers won't break it." She set the Waterford Crystal down carefully.

"If they do, let me know. The vase comes with a lifetime-replacement guarantee."

There was no use arguing. "Shall we go?"

The maître d' was the same from a month earlier. But he led them to a different table. "I hope this suits you."

The waiter came and offered them a list of nonalcoholic drinks. "The Chicago Sunset is our house nonalcoholic special. Would you like one while you wait for your appetizer?"

Preston looked to Abbie for confirmation before ordering.

"I'll have the drinks right out."

Preston reached across the table and took her hand. "A penny for your thoughts?"

"I don't think you own a penny."

"I do too." Preston dug in his pockets.

The waiter set their drinks down and left. The bartender had gone the extra mile and placed a bowtie on one, a red-ribbon rose on the other.

Preston pulled a hundred-dollar bill out of his pocket. "Wait. Let me check the other one."

Abbie sipped her drink. A hint of mango and maybe citrus of some kind.

Preston held up a quarter. "Will this do?"

"I knew you didn't have a penny."

Preston said something, but Abbie wasn't sure what. Something was wrong. She took a drink of water to clear her mouth.

Was that Felicia? The woman leaving the bar area turned and gave a little wave.

"Felicia—"

Preston dove to catch Abbie as she toppled out of her chair. Adam materialized from someplace barking orders.

No! Don't die! I should have called this off!

Alex took Preston by the shoulders. "What did she say?"

"What?"

"Right before she passed out, Abbie pointed to the bar and said something."

Preston shook his head. Why weren't they giving her CPR?

Alex got in Preston's face. "What did she say?"

"I don't know. Feil... fall... falling... no... fell se? None of that makes sense. Fell... Felicia! Why would she say my cousin's name? She is supposed to be in New York."

Alex leaped passed him. Adam appeared.

Paramedics came. Abbie looked so pale. Bodyguards he didn't recognize attempted to block patrons from taking photographs.

A man in uniform asked him a question. Preston reached for his glass of water before answering.

Adam's hand grabbed his. "Don't. The water, drink, or both may be drugged. Did you drink anything?"

Preston shook his head.

The officer spoke again. "Sir, why don't we step outside so you can answer a couple of questions."

Adam started to follow.

The officer turned on him. "I only asked Mr. Harmon to come."

Adam pulled out a card. "Adam Hastings, Hastings security. Unless Mr. Harmon is under arrest, I go where he does. May I suggest you call Detective Spencer? He is already familiar with this stalking case."

The officer glared but spoke into his radio, requesting the detective.

When they reached the outer lobby, the officer spoke again. "Mr. Harmon. Did Miss Henderson eat or drink anything other than the drinks on the table in the past hour?"

"No, not that I am aware of. But I have only been with her"—Preston consulted his watch—"for about forty minutes."

"Were you alone with Miss Henderson during that time?" asked the officer.

"Not technically. My driver, bodyguards, and surveillance cameras—one or the other was with me from the time I left my residence."

The detective arrived and conferred with the officer.

The sounds of sirens announced Abbie was en route to the hospital. Preston looked to Adam for reassurance.

"Alex is with her. Simon is looking for—"

Detective Spencer stepped out of his car and rushed into the middle of the conversation. "Mr. Hastings, I am going to guess you are already a step ahead of us. Catch me up with the short version."

Adam rubbed the back of his neck. "Working theory is Felicia Harmon was in the bar when the bartender made their drinks. Abbie saw her leaving the bar and tried to tell Preston. You may find something on the restaurant's security. There is also an exterior camera on the front door. Simon Dermot was contacted and said Felicia arrived this morning from New York, where she had been since early yesterday. She went home, but no one saw her leave her residence. However, she is not at her home now."

The detective looked from Preston to Adam and back. "I suppose you two will be useless to me until you are with her, go with Officer Simms. He'll take you to the hospital. I'll let you know if we find anything in the glasses ASAP. The doctors will need to know too."

There was something unnerving about riding in the back of the patrol car. Preston took solace in the knowledge that neither he nor Adam were handcuffed.

Adam read a text on his phone, then leaned over. "How could Felicia get out of her residence without anyone on Simon's team noticing? They have searched the mansion, and she isn't there."

"The old bootlegger tunnels."

Adam typed into his phone. "Simon's asking where the entrance is."

"The fastest way to find the secret door is to show you. Is my uncle or father around?"

Texts pinged on Adam's phone. "No, but someone named Josephine is."

"My Great-Aunt Josephine. She would know too."

The police car pulled into the bay, and the officers let Adam and Preston out. Jethro was in the waiting room. "Alex is back there with Abbie. Melanie is on her way."

Alex burst out the doors. "The doctor's kicked me out. She had a seizure. They think she was slipped both GHB and ketamine and maybe something else. I don't get it. We had eyes on the bartender the entire time he made the drinks."

"What about Felicia?" asked Preston.

Adam looked up from his phone. "She must have been in the room when we got there, but she didn't sit near the bar, so she couldn't have touched them. The bodyguard from Dallas, Peter, noticed her, but she was with a friend, and he didn't make the connection with Preston."

Preston followed the other to a corner and found a chair. "So the stalker might not be Felicia?"

Jethro's phone rang, and he left the lobby. The canned laughter of a sitcom rerun blared from the TV. Adam and Alex stared at their phones.

Jethro returned. "That was Detective Spencer. Late this afternoon Felicia came to the bar and spoke with the bartender about your date. She gave him two sets of specially decorated glasses. A frosted set of water glasses and the decorated wine glasses. She then returned to the bar, where she sat with a man she'd met on a dating app. The man said he'd never met her before, and he thought she had a crush on the bartender because she was constantly looking at him. The detective says there is still a bit of powder in her water glass. He is waiting on the results, but the on-site test was positive for GHB. The drinking glass didn't have any powder in it, but the bartender had thought the glass was dirty, then decided it was just the reflection from the glue holding the ribbon wrap on. Pending full lab results, they think the ketamine was already inside her glass."

Preston put his head in his hands. Even after Felicia started the fight at Monday's dinner, he had never suspected her. When she'd vowed to marry him when she was fourteen, they'd discussed it thoroughly. Even his mom and aunt had sat Felicia down. "I need to go call my parents. I'll be back in a few."

twenty-five

ANTISEPTIC, MACHINES BEEPING, AND VOICES. Abbie struggled to open her eyes to confirm what her other senses were telling her.

"Doctor, she is coming around."

"Miss Hastings, can you hear me?"

She forced her eyes open. A doctor smiled at her. "You are on IV and oxygen, but the worst should be over. Humans were not meant to ingest horse medicine. We are going to keep you down here for another hour or so until they find you a room for the night. The lobby is full of family here for you, plus a police detective. I'll have the nurse bring one person back to sit with you. Who would you like?"

He probably wasn't here, but she said the first name that came to her mind. "Preston."

The effort to keep her eyes open was too great, so she closed them and concentrated on breathing the oxygen coming from the plastic tube in her nose.

The door opened. Preston. Abbie hoped she had gotten the right muscles to work to smile at him.

"Hey, Abbie, how are you feeling?"

Abbie moved her left hand. "Ring. Sorry. I'll pay."

"Sweetheart, Alex took it. He gave it to me. Now, how are you?"

"Odd. My brain isn't listening—No, I mean my body isn't listening to my brain."

"Do you remember Detective Spencer?"

Abbie turned to the other man. Not sure if she nodded, she said, "Yes."

The detective stepped closer to the bed. "I have a few questions for you."

"Stalker is Felicia... left the bar." She closed her eyes and willed her brain and her mouth to get in sync. "I tried to tell—sorry, I broken."

"Take your time. Why do you think it's Felicia?" asked the detective.

Abbie took a few breaths and allowed her mind to put several pictures in order. "She sat next to me when the snake got in my salad, long prayer. Last year at some event, Patrick Vonn insinuated he was more than a bodyguard to his client. He often worked for her." Abbie paused for a breath. "After the bridal shower, she told me I didn't belong in her world. Texts said the same thing. But her smile when she left the bar..." She shuddered. Preston took her hand.

"What about her smile?" prompted the detective.

"Triumphant. And the finger wave. She should have told Preston hello. She is your cousin. I don't understand."

"Mr. Harmon, do you have any theories?"

Preston stood but didn't let go of Abbie's hand. "Felicia is my aunt's daughter, though not my uncle's. When she was ten or twelve, she realized that since we weren't blood relations, she could marry me. Everyone told her a relationship would be scandalous. Three years ago, when she graduated college, she tried unsuccessfully to seduce me. I thought she was joking. I know I hurt her feelings, but she seemed to have gotten over it. She even apologized and said she was wrong. Since then she never mentioned—"

"I understand, Mr. Harmon. I'll let you know if we have any further questions." The detective left the room.

Preston sat back down. "I should have listened to you when you asked about her at first."

Abbie tried to move closer to him, but she was too tangled in wires and cords. "Preston, it's okay. We got her, and you are safe. My job is done."

Preston sat for several minutes, or maybe seconds. Time wasn't moving right. "Your entire family is in the lobby. I had better give your mom and Alex a turn." He stood. "Bye, Abbie, and thank you."

Mom came in next and filled the seat Preston had been in. "The detective called. They caught her."

"Good." Abbie closed her eyes. "He left, didn't he."

"I think so."

Abbie opened her eyes enough to see her mother. "I told you so." She closed her eyes again and waited to fade back into oblivion, where she wouldn't feel her heart.

3:00 a.m.

The clock didn't want to move any faster. Preston went to his closet and pulled out a clean shirt, then called security to let them know he was leaving and would be driving himself.

The house was quiet, so he went to grab something from the kitchen.

Mum sat at the table stirring her tea.

"Mum, what are you doing up?"

"I was waiting for you."

"Why?"

"I wanted to see if you are as smart as I hope you are." She lifted a plate. "Muffin?"

Preston took one. "I don't know if I am or not, but I need to see her. So maybe that makes me stupid. Love you, Mum." He kissed her cheek and opened the back door.

"No, son, you are not stupid."

Preston didn't turn to respond.

The hospital hallway lights were set on dim. Only the light above the nurse's station shone brightly. Preston didn't stop as he headed for the room. It was easy enough to find with Alex sitting out in the hallway.

"What are you doing here?" Alex shifted in his seat.

"I need to see her." He couldn't explain what he didn't understand.

Alex stood. "Job's over. You left."

"I needed to go deal with the family. You guys needed to see her. I took a turn."

"You left her."

"With you and your brothers and your parents. May I go in?"

"So you can leave her again? You know she asks for you every time she wakes up."

"Then I want to be here when she wakes up again."

Alex shifted his weight but kept blocking the door. "I don't think so. The way I see it, the only person in this family you are going to see is me, in a ring, like you promised."

The door opened behind Alex, and Jethro stepped out. "What is going on? Oh, Preston, it's you. What are you doing here at four in the morning?"

Alex moved only far enough for his father to get out of the doorway. "He had an appointment to set up with me."

"You came to see Alex?" Jethro's eyes twinkled.

"No, I came to see Abbie."

"Do you love my daughter?"

"I think she should be the first one to hear that from me."

Jethro opened the door and bowed slightly. "You may want to wait to tell her. The doctors said she will probably not remember much that happens for the next few hours."

"Thank you." Preston started to walk into the room.

Jethro stopped him with a hand. "It is customary to speak with the father at some point. I'll expect you in my office before the end of the day."

Preston nodded and walked into the room.

twenty-six

"TESSA! AND ARACELI! YOU'RE BOTH here." Abbie hugged Araceli. "Mrs. Evans, I thought you would be on your honeymoon still. Didn't you get the memo? This isn't a real hen party."

"You think I cared? Any chance to see y'all. Starting July first, I'll be in Haiti for three months." Araceli glanced at Tessa. "Other than the last weekend in August, when I'll be in New York."

"Did you guys hear that? She's only been married to the Texan for two weeks and already she is saying 'y'all,'" said Candace in a passable accent.

"I think I was supposed to say 'all y'all.' I still don't quite get it." Araceli used a horrific accent, sending them all into peals of laughter.

Abbie stopped first. "Hey, no laughter around the pregnant lady." She turned to Mandy, who sat on the couch.

"Go ahead. Laugh away. I reached the magical thirty-sixth week today. I can walk and sit up and go places, although the doctor would prefer I don't ride any lawn mowers. I assured her it wouldn't be a problem in the city."

Candace put a tiara on Abbie. "I say we let the festivities begin!"

Abbie took the crown off. "But there isn't a wedding tomorrow. We caught Felicia, and even if we hadn't, the wedding would have been fake."

Mandy stood and picked up the plastic crown. "But you said he was there when you woke up. He said he loved you."

Abbie sank into a chair. "I don't know what he said. Everything is kind of blurry in my memory. I'm fairly sure my brothers weren't dressed up like giant fruit and dancing around my room, but I remember that, too." Abby counted on her fingers. "But I know for one, I don't have a ring. Two, the evening news on all four major stations reported Felicia was his stalker and I was an undercover bodyguard. And three, I haven't seen or heard from him since he left the hospital this morning to go 'take care of things.'"

Zoe sat down opposite her. "Two of the newscasters were disappointed the engagement wasn't real."

"Probably because they will have to find something else for tomorrow night's show's feel-good moment."

Candace rapped her knuckles on the table. "I hereby call an emergency Thursday evening meeting of the Friday Night Art Society. Let the festivities begin."

"Presents first!" Mandy handed Abbie a wrapped box.

The Canon was the same model Daniel had purchased for the university. Abbie knew the $80K price tag well. "That is too much. I can't—"

"Don't you dare say you can't take it, Abigale Annette Hastings. I'll have you know you need this if you are to be the official photographer of Miss-I'm-Waiting-Till July." Mandy patted her baby bump.

Abbie hugged Mandy. "Fine, then, I'd better keep it, but perhaps I should test it out tonight."

"Good thing I charged the battery."

Two hours later the room was a litter of pizza plates, ice cream bowls, and toilet-paper super-hero capes. An oft-watched chick-flick played on the big screen.

Abbie's phone pinged. Preston. Abbie handed the phone to Mandy. "I can't look."

Mandy read the message and handed the phone back. "I don't understand. Are you doing a photo shoot tomorrow?"

Abbie took the phone back.

Still have Knickerbocker booked. Perfect place for a photo shoot. Please be there at 1:00 p.m. Bring the dress. Plan on two hours.

Abbie read the message out loud. "I agreed to model the dress for a magazine shoot. I guess with the place still booked, he may as well get some use out of it." Her hand flew to her hair. "Oh no! I have roots showing!"

"No problem. Who is in for a spa morning?" Mandy typed into her phone. Everyone raised their hand. "Okay, then, six appointments starting at 8:00 a.m."

Zoe set down her popcorn bowl. "How did you do that?"

Mandy smiled. "Sometimes being Mrs. Daniel Crawford III pays off."

Abbie texted Preston back. **I'll be there.**

Preston paced the lobby of the Knickerbocker Hotel, even though Mandy Crawford had texted him twice to reassure him Abbie would be there and the plans he'd set in place were on schedule. He looked over to the photographer. His phone vibrated. **One block.**

The black limo pulled up, and Abbie got out, followed by five of her friends, including a slightly waddling Mandy. The doorman offered to take the dress, but Abbie refused. Preston couldn't help but smile.

The women looked around the lobby. Abbie spotted him almost immediately and walked in his direction. The friend with the brightly colored hair whisked the dress bag out of Abbie's arms. Her steps slowed as she looked back and realized her friends were not following her. Mandy nodded at Abbie and made a shooing motion.

Preston closed the gap, offered her his arm, and led her over to a divan on the far side of the lobby.

"Is something wrong?" Abbie's eyes darted around the room.

"Well, pretty much everything, but I would like to fix that." He dropped to one knee. Abbie covered her mouth exactly the way she had the first time he knelt before her. "Abigale Annette Hastings, I've learned so much from you this month about love and life and friendship. I told you this yesterday morning, but apparently you don't remember. Abbie, I love you. Will you make everything right in my life and marry me?"

Abbie kept her hand over her mouth and nodded.

"This is the real thing this time. I need to hear you say it."

She dropped her hand and clasped his. "Yes! Yes!"

Across the lobby, her friends clapped.

Preston stood and took Abbie in his arms. "I have come to believe in short engagements. Do you think two hours is long enough, or should we make it three?"

"One?"

Preston laughed. "We need to wait for our parents and the minister."

When Preston bent and kissed her lightly, Abbie leaned in to him to bring them closer. On his seventy-fifth wedding anniversary, he knew he would recall this kiss. It was the perfect first kiss. (After all, the other one didn't count.)

epilogue

WHEN THE BAND STARTED PLAYING, Preston took Abbie's hand, pulled her onto the empty dance floor, and led her expertly through the waltz. Abbie wondered how many of her brothers wanted to storm the dance floor and separate them. Even though they had all stood up with them during the ceremony, she wasn't sure they fully supported the quick marriage.

"Adam and Alex are glaring. Should I be worried?" Preston led her in a turn.

Laughter bubbled up. "I don't know. Should you be?"

"Maybe." He kissed her quickly. Abbie pulled him back into a lingering kiss. She was quite sure she could spend the rest of her life happily in his arms.

The music changed, and their parents joined them. In time the dance floor was filled. Her brothers took turns asking her for a dance. Alan and Andrew wished her the best. Adam tried to. Alex growled out dire threats.

Back in her husband's arms—she liked the sound of that, *husband*—back in her husband's arms, she danced through the crowd, passing Daniel and Mandy, who had come to a full stop.

Mandy shrieked.

The music stopped.

The dancers stopped.

Abbie's heart stopped.

Abbie went for her gun only to remember she wasn't wearing it under her voluminous skirts. Alex hurried to the Crawfords' side. Mandy leaned heavily on Daniel, her face pale, a puddle spreading on the floor beneath her.

Daniel spoke loudly. "Sorry about this, Abbie, but it seems our little one doesn't want to miss out on the party." He turned to Alex. "Now would be an excellent time to call for our car."

Mandy grasped Abbie's arm. "Sorry to spoil your reception."

"Nonsense." Abbie let Candace replace her by Mandy's side.

She turned to Preston and wondered if she were about to start the first argument of their marriage. "I made Mandy a promise that I would be her bodyguard when the baby came. I know the timing is bad, but—"

"Are you asking to delay our honeymoon?" Preston raised a brow.

Abbie bit her lip and nodded.

"Will this be your last job as a bodyguard?"

"Officially, yes. It doesn't make sense for me to be a bodyguard, when I need one." She didn't tell him she would never stop guarding him or that someday their children might have the only mom in the PTA with a concealed-carry license.

Preston whispered his conditions for letting her miss out on their wedding night in her ear. Abbie felt the blush rise. She nodded.

"Then I suggest we go get you changed."

"We?"

"I'm not going to miss helping my bride out of her dress, even if it is so she can spend our wedding night someplace other than by my side." Preston's roguish grin sent a delightful chill down her spine. She hoped for a quick delivery.

Two stories spent the weekend competing for social media most shared:

Amanda and Daniel Crawford III welcomed their daughter Joy Dawn into the world. #BabyJoy

Preston Harmon and his new bride Abigale, end reception early and postpone honeymoon. #PrestonWed

Of course, both stories left out that Joy was born soon after midnight and that the Harmons left on their honeymoon only six hours later than initially planned.

The End

acknowledgments

As always my books need a lot of help to get from my head and into your hands. Photography is art, and perhaps the only art I have written about so far that I haven't learned. But I did grow up with a father who had a dark room and a Hasselblad camera.

Tammy and Nanette are so willing to help make all my projects better and to read things so many times even in late night texts. I would never make it through a day without Sally and Cindy whose advice keeps me going. Thank you wonderful ladies. And to Araceli for letting me use her name.

Thanks also to Michele at Eschler Editing for the edits and finding oh so many little things to fix; any mistakes left in this book are not her fault. Nor are my excellent proofreaders to be blamed. Thank you ladies and gents!

My family, for sharing their home with the fictional characters who often got fed better than they did. And my husband who encourages me every crazy step of the way and puts up with all my messy spreadsheets.

And to my Father in Heaven for putting these wonderful people, and any I may have forgotten to mention, in my life. I am grateful for every experience and blessing I have been granted.

about the author

LORIN GRACE WAS BORN IN Colorado and has been moving around the country ever since, living in eight states and several imaginary worlds. She graduated from Brigham Young University with a degree in Graphic Design.

Currently she lives in northern Utah with her husband, four children, and a dog who is insanely jealous of her laptop. When not writing, Lorin enjoys creating graphics, visiting historical sites, museums, and reading.

LORIN IS AN ACTIVE MEMBER of the League of Utah Writers and was awarded Honorable Mention in their 2016 creative writing contest short romance story category. Her debut novel, *Waking Lucy,* was awarded a 2017 Recommended Read award in the LUW Published book contest. In 2018 the first book in this series, Mending Fences with the Billionaire, also received a Recommended Read award.

You can learn more about her, and sign up for her writers club at loringrace.com or at Facebook: LorinGraceWriter